WORRIED TO DEATH

"You don't think we could have done anything to prevent it?" said Sue.

The doctor shook her head. "There was nothing anybody could have done."

But Sue still looked anxious. "I wonder if it was anything to do with the strain of moving into a different flat."

"It might have contributed," admitted Dr. Mercer, "but she wanted to move, and if it hadn't been that it could have been something else."

"Could worry cause a heart attack?"

"Was Mrs. Graham worried about anything?" asked Dr. Mercer, giving Sue a keen glance.

"She never said so, but I had a feeling that she was. I'd got to know her quite well, you see, and she was sort of different lately. Not exactly discontented, but sort of . . . sort of . . ."

Sue waved her hands about helplessly. "Oh, I don't know. It sounds so silly, but it was almost as if she had a premonition that she was going to die . . ."

Charter Books by Anna Clarke

SOON SHE MUST DIE
WE THE BEREAVED
ONE OF US MUST DIE
DESIRE TO KILL
LETTER FROM THE DEAD
(coming in January 1989)

ANNA CLARKE

DESIRE TO KILL

CHARTER BOOKS, NEW YORK

This Charter book contains the complete
text of the original hardcover edition.
It has been completely reset in a typeface
designed for easy reading, and was printed
from new film.

DESIRE TO KILL

A Charter Book/published by arrangement with
Doubleday, a division of Bantam, Doubleday, Dell
Publishing Group, Inc.

PRINTING HISTORY
Doubleday edition published 1982
Charter edition/November 1988

ISBN: 1-55773-118-7

Charter Books are published by The Berkley Publishing Group,
200 Madison Avenue, New York, New York 10016.
The name "CHARTER" and the "C" logo
are trademarks belonging to Charter Communications, Inc.

PRINTED IN THE UNITED STATES OF AMERICA

10 9 8 7 6 5 4 3 2 1

Amy Langford had never before felt ill will towards any other creature. That was what she told herself on the evening of the first day that she came to live at Digby Hall. And it was on that very first day that she began to experience those feelings of violent rage and hatred of all the people around her that grew more and more intense and less and less controllable as the weeks and months went by.

There were six apartments in the Hall, each one completely self-contained, but the residents all met in the dining room for a hot meal at midday. The woman sitting next to Amy greeted her in what Amy thought was rather an offhand manner on the first day, and to show her up, Amy responded with a very polite remark about the pleasant view from the dining-room window.

"It's nice, isn't it," said the neighbour, who was called Miss Pick. "When the trees are bare in winter we can actually get a glimpse of the sea."

Amy allowed a little sigh to escape her. "I'm afraid I've been spoilt," she said. "There is a most wonderful sea view from the sun lounge in my bungalow." She paused, but the neighbour said nothing. "You can imagine yourself on the deck of a ship," she went on. "My husband designed it himself. He was an architect. A very clever man."

Miss Pick said, "Oh really?" and continued to eat her steak and kidney pie with what Amy thought was most unladylike enthusiasm.

"Of course I wouldn't dream of putting the bungalow up for sale," she said, picking delicately at her own portion of pie. Actually, it was rather nice, but as a silent rebuke to her neighbour's greed she decided to leave a little of it. "I only agreed to give Digby Hall a trial because it was so highly recommended, and my son thought the bungalow was becoming too much for me. Unfortunately, he can't be with me as much as he would like to because he designs exhibitions for big firms and his work takes him all over the world. But I am only to stay here as long as I am happy. He was most emphatic about that."

"I expect you'll like it here," said Miss Pick briskly. "They give you one good meal a day, and if you don't want to be sociable you can keep to your own flat the rest of the time. And there's shops five minutes away and a good bus service into Brighton from the end of the road, and the warden and her husband are delightful. Couldn't find a nicer young couple. Can't think how they have the patience to look after all us old crocks."

Miss Pick gave a laugh that sounded to Amy rather more like a snort. Actually, she looked rather like a horse, with her angular features and untidy white hair. Not a very friendly person, thought Amy, not quite what one would have expected in these highly recommended apartments for retired professional people. However, she must not expect too much at first. She would give Miss Pick another chance. She tried again.

"Of course we could have advertised for a housekeeper-companion to live with me. My son would never dream of letting the expense stand in the way if it would make me happy. But I didn't quite like the idea of taking somebody into my own home. There are such odd people about nowadays, aren't there?"

Surely Miss Pick would respond to this opening, thought

Amy. It was very rude of her not to show more interest in Amy's situation and more sympathy with her for having to think of taking a stranger into her home, but Miss Pick must be some sort of a lady or she would not be in Digby Hall at all. Even if she was not going to be kind and understanding, at least it might be possible to have a comfortable little conversation with her about how dreadful everything was nowadays.

"Oh? do you think so?" said Miss Pick. "I don't suppose people are any more odd nowadays than they always have been."

Amy Langford found this so offensive that she very nearly choked on a piece of her apple crumble. It was a very good apple crumble, almost as good as she could make herself, but her neighbour's rudeness completely spoilt it for her. She could not turn her back on Miss Pick because they were seated side by side at the long table, but she could at least talk instead to her other neighbour.

This was the warden, Mrs. Merry, and she certainly looked a merry little thing, with her smiling face and bright brown eyes. Too young to be in such a position, though, and surely she ought to be dressed in a more dignified manner when she sat at the end of the table, and not in shabby old trousers and what looked like a man's shirt. At least she was friendly, though. Amy had to admit that.

"I do so hope you are going to be happy with us, Mrs. Langford," she said. "You will tell me, won't you, if you want anything done in your flat. Bob will fix that curtain rail for you tomorrow, and if there's anything else . . ."

Oh yes, she was certainly helpful enough, but after all, that was what she was paid for, and Amy still thought it would have been more suitable to have an older woman in the job. However, any sympathetic ear was better than none, and Amy was just about to talk about her bungalow which had been designed by her clever architect husband and about how her son only wanted her to be happy, when Mrs. Merry turned to her other neighbour and gave her the same beaming smile and asked about her arthritis.

Amy could have wept. But it would be no use to cry just

now, with so many people present, eight of them in all,
including herself; six residents and the warden and her
husband. Their faces became blurred. The noise of their
chatter faded away. Amy thought she was going to faint.
She had had rather a lot of these bad turns before it was
finally decided that she should come to Digby Hall. Several
times Jonathan had had to fly back from abroad because of
them. When he had said, "You can't go on like this,
Mother," her heart had leapt with joy because she thought
he was going to suggest giving up his job and getting one
nearer home and coming to live with her. But instead he had
said . . .

Amy tried not to think of it. She would certainly burst
into tears if she remembered that day. She had cried a great
deal but it had had no effect. There always had been a
certain hardness about Jonathan, her own son. Not like his
dear father, who would never have allowed her to suffer.

The strange voices became louder once more, the strange
faces once again took shape. Nobody else seemed to have
noticed the agony she was going through. Nobody ever
would notice again; nobody would ever care again how
much she suffered. The thought was so terrible that it dried
her eyes. It was like a searing pain. She sat paralysed with
it, and when at last it had died away she saw quite clearly all
these hateful people around her who cared nothing for her
sufferings. The false smiling face of Mrs. Merry, and the
dirty-looking young man with long hair at the other end of
the table who was her husband. The little twisted figure
opposite of the woman who had arthritis, and next to her
one of the two men among the residents, a balding, fat, red-
faced elderly man who looked as if he drank too much. Next
to him was the big woman with the dyed hair and the
raucous laugh. Opposite her, beyond Miss Pick on the same
side of the table as Amy, was the other male resident, quite
a distinguished-looking white-haired man whom Amy had
hoped to sit next to but who had told her, courteously of
course because he was certainty a gentleman, that the centre
place on that side of the table was Miss Pick's.

That was the moment when hatred took the place of pain.

Amy didn't even know all their names yet but she hated them. Miss Pick was the worst. She was leaning across the table now to talk to the fat man opposite, uttering her horse-like laugh at something the man said. Disgusting. At her age. Behaving like a silly girl trying to get a husband. Well, if she hadn't succeeded by now she had better give up trying. But some women never learnt what appealed to men. Perhaps Miss Pick was not quite right in the head. Sometimes these frustrated spinsters did go that way. She would be jealous, of course, of Amy Langford's good looks and her beautiful bungalow and the clever husband she had had and the son who only wanted her to be happy.

Thinking about Miss Pick's jealousy helped Amy through the rest of that first day. On the second day she found herself sitting on the terrace next to the lady with arthritis, whose name was Mrs. Graham. The woman with the raucous laugh had been collected by a young couple in a large car and driven away. The red-faced man had not yet put in an appearance. Miss Pick was down at the bottom of the garden with young Bob Merry, supposedly helping him mend the fence; and the distinguished-looking man, after greeting Amy politely, had retired to the other end of the terrace and hidden himself behind *The Times*.

For want of any better company, Amy decided to talk to Mrs. Graham. It was not very pleasant to have to look at her frail and twisted body, but in other respects Amy found her not a bad person to talk to. Her face was kind and gentle and she had a pleasant low voice. She had also been married, so there was no question of an old maid's jealousy.

"Lovely morning," said Amy, smiling at Mrs. Graham for a moment and then leaning back and shutting her eyes as if against the sun. That was a good enough excuse for not seeing the poor crooked back and the knotted fingers.

"Beautiful," agreed the other, "and the weatherman has promised us some more."

"Have you been here long?" was Amy's next venture. She was longing to talk about herself, but some instinct told her that it would be better to wait a little.

"About three years," said Mrs. Graham.

Three years! How could anybody endure this place for three years! But then of course, poor thing, thought Amy, she probably had no choice, being crippled like that.

"It's a nice old house," she said guardedly, hoping to work her way round to a comparison with her own beautiful modern bungalow.

"Oh it is indeed!" cried Mrs. Graham with enthusiasm. "And it's been so well converted into flats. They've kept the proportions of the rooms and the ceiling mouldings, and the essential structural alterations have been done with real respect for the overall effect. The balconies, for instance. A most unusual feature in a house of that period, but most attractive."

"I've got a balcony," said Amy, "and a window opening onto it, but there's not room to sit out."

"Oh, they are only meant to be decorative," said Mrs. Graham. "Although they can be used for window boxes to good effect. That is one of the many things I like about the house—the blending of the brickwood and the natural beauties around it."

Mrs. Graham continued to talk about Digby Hall for several minutes more and Amy listened in amazement. It might also have been Philip speaking. Not that he had ever talked much about his work at home, but occasionally he would hold forth about some building or other, and Amy would say, "Yes, dear," or "Really? Isn't that interesting," just to make him feel that she cared about his enthusiasms.

"My husband was an architect," she said when Mrs. Graham had finished speaking at last.

"Was he?" said the kindly, gentle voice. "I'm so sorry, but I'm afraid I didn't catch your name."

"Langford. My husband's name was Philip."

"Well, isn't that interesting!"

There was such warmth in Mrs. Graham's tone that Amy roused herself to look at her. She was smiling, a very sweet smile, and there was quite a sparkle in the faded blue eyes. For a few moments Amy felt gratified. At any rate, one human being in this horrible unfriendly place had turned upon her a look of genuine good will.

"Philip Langford," Mrs. Graham was saying. "I never met him myself, but I certainly remember my husband speaking of him. He was an architect too."

"Was he really? Isn't that strange!"

Amy tried her best to sound as enthusiastic as her companion. A Mr. Graham. Had Philip ever mentioned a Mr. Graham? She could not remember. She never remembered much of what Philip said. It wasn't usually very interesting. But if Mr. Graham had ever been invited to the bungalow she would certainly have remembered, because she always noticed at once whether Philip's friends were going to be polite and considerate to her or whether they were going to start talking straightaway about things that did not interest her. She could not recall a Mr. Graham in either category and this made her annoyed, not with herself but with Mrs. Graham, because it put her at a disadvantage that Mrs. Graham should have heard of her husband while she had not heard of Mrs. Graham's.

The comforting feeling that somebody was at last paying proper attention to her began to fade. Mrs. Graham's next remark caused it to vanish even more rapidly.

"I always wanted to be an architect myself," she was saying, "but in my young days it was not easy for a woman, and my parents had set their minds to my becoming a teacher. They never knew how much I disliked it, but it was some consolation, after I married, to be with someone who could teach me a little of what I had missed."

Amy could think of nothing to say to this at all. The conversation seemed to be getting further and further away from anything with which she felt at home. She could hardly say, "Yes, dear," if Mrs. Graham were to make learned remarks about architecture, nor did she feel at all inclined to keep saying, "Really? How very interesting," to a crippled old woman whom she scarcely knew. Philip had been her husband and therefore had a right to be boring, but Mrs. Graham had no claim to any such deference.

Amy felt that she was not going to like Mrs. Graham any more than she liked Miss Pick, but actually it was the sound

of the latter's voice, quite near at hand, that gave her an
excuse to change the subject.

"Oh look," she cried. "Miss Pick and Mr. Merry have
moved round to the gate now." She lowered her voice. "Do
you think Mr. Merry really wants her to help him? I should
think he'd manage better by himself."

Mrs. Graham did not follow up this invitation to criticise
Miss Pick, but took the remark quite seriously. "I dare say
he could manage by himself," she said after a moment's
consideration, "but I think it's making the job easier to have
somebody to hold the staves."

Amy could have hit her. Then she suddenly thought how
dreadful it was to feel as if you could hit a crippled little old
lady, and that made her dislike Mrs. Graham more than
ever.

"I think I'll stroll round the garden a little," she said,
getting up from her chair. "The sun's getting rather too hot
for me."

"I hope you will have pleasure in the garden, Mrs.
Langford," said Mrs. Graham, "and I hope you are going
to be as happy at Digby Hall as I have always been myself."

It took all Amy's self-control to make a polite response.

At the far end of the terrace the distinguished-looking
man was still reading *The Times*. Amy contrived to brush
against the newspaper very slightly as she passed.

"I'm so sorry," she said. "Did I disturb you?"

"Good morning," he said, lowering the paper a couple of
inches and glancing up at her with a faint smile. "Lovely
morning, isn't it?"

"Beautiful," she replied, and then could think of nothing
more to say.

The faint smile remained on his face but he spoke no
more. Perhaps he is shy, she said to herself as she walked
on; sometimes these very clever people are.

The path she was on led round the side of the house. She
did not particularly want to go in that direction, but if she
turned back now it would look as if she had deliberately set
out to speak to the man behind *The Times*, so she walked
on. Perhaps there would be a chance to talk to him later.

After all, men were always easier to get on with than women, and a fine-looking man like that would surely be more appreciative of a well-groomed woman than the envious Miss Pick or the odd Mrs. Graham had been.

By the time she had come out onto the lawn at the front of the house Amy was deep in a daydream about the man behind *The Times* and she was quite startled to hear a cultured male voice near at hand.

"Hullo, Mrs. Langford. Going to explore our woodlands?"

It was the red-faced plump man, and he was gesturing towards the shrubbery at the far side of the slope of grass.

Amy felt herself flushing. It was partly in annoyance at being taken unawares, partly in recollection of her daydream, which had got rather out of control. She muttered something about finding the sun rather too hot, and the fat man told her there was a nice shady seat beyond the lilac bushes.

"I'm Dr. Cunningham, by the way," he added. "George, if you like. Sue Merry did introduce us yesterday, I believe, but one never remembers names when one is settling into a strange place."

Amy was surprised yet again. He had spoken quite kindly and had actually remembered her name. And although he was not much to look at, the title "Doctor" had a reassuring ring.

"I'm glad we've got a doctor in the house," she said with a smile.

Perhaps after all it was worth taking trouble over him. The good-looking man might well turn out to be as unsatisfactory as the women, and in any case it would be nice to cut out that stupid Miss Pick, who had been making sheep's eyes across the table at Dr. Cunningham yesterday at lunchtime.

"Ah, I'm off duty now," he replied. "I am a medical doctor, I confess, but such skill as I ever had has gone very rusty."

"So we mustn't come to you with our aches and pains?"

"No, indeed, that you must not. You must take them to

Dr. Mercer, who pays us all a weekly visit and emergency calls as required. She is a delightful person and looks after us very well."

"Oh." Amy made no attempt to hide her dismay. "A lady doctor?"

"A lady doctor," repeated Dr. George Cunningham gravely.

"Well, I don't suppose I shall have much need of her services," said Amy recovering herself. "I am perfectly well."

"I'm glad to hear it, Mrs. Langford. I hope you may long remain so. We shall meet at lunch. Au revoir."

He made her an awkward little bow and moved on. Amy continued her walk towards the shrubbery and found the seat under the big lilac bush. Some of the blooms had faded but there were still quite a lot of sweetly scented sprays. It was indeed a cool and pleasant spot, secluded but not too isolated. Amy shut her eyes. She thought she might be going to cry, but no tears came. They seldom did when she was by herself, for what was the use of solitary weeping? It brought you nothing but a headache.

Amy opened her eyes and stared at the overripe lilacs. What was the matter with her? Was she going to have one of those dizzy turns again? For a moment she felt as if she was, and was overcome by panic and despair. She would have to send for Jonathan. He must come at once, even though it meant flying home from Rome. Or was it Holland this week? She could not remember. She would have to telephone his London office, and that horrible secretary would answer and would say it was impossible to get hold of him, and she, his own mother, would have to beg and plead and weep and threaten until at last the wretched girl admitted that there was a phone number she could ring.

And as soon as she knew Jonathan was coming she would feel better, and he would never believe how ill she had felt, and he would blame her for interrupting his work and would suggest that she should go and live in some place where there would always be people about and she would be looked after when she was ill.

But no. She was forgetting. That had already happened, and she was at this place now. Digby Hall. If she had one of those dizzy turns now, nobody would send for Jonathan. They would send for Dr. Mercer, the lady doctor. Whatever use would she be to Amy? Just about as much use as all these horrible people in this horrible place.

And yet she wanted to be friendly. Philip always used to say what a good hostess she was. Even Jonathan admitted that their dinner parties went well. The secret was to look after the men, to make sure that they had enough to eat and somebody to listen to them. The women could look after themselves. There was no need to bother with women when you had a devoted husband and a son who said he only wanted you to be happy.

She always used to be so good with men. What had gone wrong? This red-faced man she had been talking to just now—Dr. Cunningham. There had been nothing wrong there, had there? He had spoken very kindly and then they had talked quite happily, the sort of talk she understood and enjoyed, a little bit of a joke, nothing odd or unexpected, and then suddenly it had no longer seemed to be all right.

Perhaps she was imagining it. After all, he had said, "See you at lunch," which must surely mean he was looking forward to seeing her again. Perhaps he was worried that Miss Pick might see them talking together and be jealous. That was much more likely. Amy felt a little better when she had decided on this explanation. That ridiculous Miss Pick. Fancy imagining that she had anything to appeal to any man! Amy Langford would show her.

The more she thought about Miss Pick's discomfiture and distress, the better Amy felt. And she didn't have any unpleasant feelings of guilt, such as had overcome her when her irritation with Mrs. Graham had actually made her feel as if she would like to strike the crippled lady. Miss Pick had not even managed to get herself a husband and she deserved no mercy.

Amy went up to her own apartment, which was on the first floor, before lunch, changed into a pretty pale-blue

summer frock and arranged her hair and face with great
care. She felt doubly satisfied with her appearance when she
found that Miss Pick had come in to lunch in her old
gardening clothes. The absence of the raucous-voiced
woman, whose name was Mrs. Ramsden, also seemed to be
to Amy's advantage, for she found that she had been moved
into Mrs. Ramsden's place, opposite the fine-looking man,
with young Mr. Merry at the head of the table on her left,
and Dr. Cunningham on her right.

This meant that she was in the midst of the three men,
whereas the other three women present were bunched
together at the other end of the table. It was a most
unorthodox arrangement for a social occasion, but in the
circumstances it suited Amy very well. The first course—a
melon cocktail—was already there in their places.

"Very refreshing," said Amy to Dr. Cunningham. "Just
right for a hot day."

He agreed. "Did you find your shady seat?" he added.

"Oh yes. It was lovely. Just like you said it would be."

Amy smiled at him and then quickly glanced across and
along the table to make sure that Miss Pick had noticed. She
was disconcerted and disappointed to find that Miss Pick
was not there.

"Oh," she exclaimed, turning to Bob Merry, who
seemed to be rather isolated because the fine-looking man
was sitting silent, not talking to him, "is Miss Pick not
well?"

Perhaps she had strained her back, skipping about in that
silly manner and pretending to mend fences. The thought of
Miss Pick with a strained back gave Amy a lot of
satisfaction. She fixed her features into an expression of
concern and waited for Bob Merry to reply.

"She's fine as far as I know," he said. "She's only gone
to help Sue bring in the mutton. It saves making several
journeys. Here they are. No, it isn't lamb. It's pork. I do
hope you like pork, Mrs. Langford. If not, then Sue or I can
easily rustle you up an omelette."

Mr. Merry's attentiveness only went a little way towards
easing Amy's chagrin at the sight of Miss Pick cheerfully

handing out plates and dumping dishes of vegetables on the table. She looked at her own plate and felt as if its contents would choke her, although only a moment ago she had looked forward to the meal with a good appetite.

"You don't like pork," said Bob Merry with concern. "Let me fix you something else. Some eggs? Cold beef?"

He was pushing back his chair, ready to run to do what she asked.

Amy felt that she ought to be gratified, but instead she only felt more and more miserable and furious, all the more so because she could not understand why. The young man with the long hair was only behaving in the courteous and attentive manner in which Philip had always behaved to her. And Jonathan too. And Amy's father in her childhood so long ago. And her brother, long since dead. And all friends and neighbours except those rude and churlish people whom Philip would not have in the house because they upset her.

The young man with the long hair was only giving Mrs. Langford her due. At a word from her he would rush off to do his best to please her, and the whole table would see that he was doing so. It was the sort of situation that Amy had always rather enjoyed when they dined with business friends of Philip's, or even at home, when she had provided a dish that she did not eat herself and Philip had got up just as she had finished bringing it in and had said: "You sit down, old girl. I'll fetch you your baby meal."

Everyone would then exclaim: "Oh, what a pity! Can't you eat this goulash? It's so delicious." Amy had always felt very much the centre of attention, in the most gratifying way.

Then why was it all wrong now? She said to Bob Merry, "No, it's all right, thanks. I don't dislike pork. I just don't feel very hungry. Perhaps it's the weather."

He sat down again and began to talk about the odd jobs he was going to do for her in her apartment. Nobody could have been more attentive and helpful, and yet there was no joy in it for her at all. She could not get up any interest in the big room that Mrs. Graham admired so much, nor in the well-fitted bathroom, and the little kitchen where the residents prepared their meals apart from the lunch that they all ate together.

"I'm afraid I won't be able to do anything this evening," said Bob Merry, "because I'm out at my Open University tutorial class, but I'll come round tomorrow afternoon if it suits you."

"That would be very kind," said Amy, picking at the food on her plate and wishing Bob Merry to the devil. The very phrase formed itself in her mind, and yet again she was surprised and appalled at the amount of fury in her thoughts and feelings.

After a while it died down a little and she remembered that she had intended to charm Dr. Cunningham in order to spite Miss Pick. She turned towards him: he was deep in conversation with Mrs. Graham at his other side. Miss Pick and the warden, young Mrs. Merry, were laughing together in the most silly childish manner, which left only Bob Merry, whom she felt she could no longer endure, and the fine-looking old man who spoke so little.

Amy summoned up a look of friendly interest and leaned across the table. "Did the terrace get too hot for you too?" she asked.

The man gave his faint smile but did not speak.

"Mr. Horder is very deaf," said Dr. Cunningham's voice in Amy's ear. "He likes people to talk to him and sometimes he can guess what you have said, but more often he can't."

"I see. Thank you for telling me," said Amy.

It took every bit of her remaining self-control to get the words out calmly. The disappointment and disillusion had risen to the same sort of searing pain as she had experienced at this table the previous day.

Very deaf. So that was the answer to the mystery of the distinguished-looking man whom her daydream had placed in the role of protector and admirer of Amy Langford. With such a champion to laugh at her little jokes, listen to her troubles and marvel at all the glories of her former life, open the door for her, hold out her chair for her, and generally make it plain to all the others that one person, at least, treasured and valued her, why then, even life at Digby Hall might become tolerable.

Very deaf. Amy absorbed this information as if it had been a personal insult to herself.

Very deaf. Just like any other decrepit old person. Just like that tiresome neighbour of hers in the bungalow who would never even try to hear what she was saying, but who always seemed to understand well enough when his wife called him in from the garden.

Very deaf. It was unbearable. One after another her hopes were being dashed. Every one of these six people sitting round the table had let her down. Not one of them seemed to have the slightest idea that she, Amy Langford, was something very special, to be cherished and protected like fine porcelain. Her father had known; Philip had known; but Jonathan—

At the thought of what Jonathan, her very own son, had said, Amy felt herself grow dizzy again. She must have shown visible signs of her distress this time because she heard Dr. Cunningham ask if she was all right.

"I think it must be the heat," she heard her own voice saying. "I don't think I feel quite up to the lemon mousse . . . it looks quite delicious . . . but if you would excuse me . . ."

She was on her feet and making her way out of the room, hardly knowing how she had got there. The pain was unbelievable and seemed to be all over her at once. It was a marvel that she could move. Perhaps she was having a heart attack. Except that her doctor's examination before she came to Digby Hall had shown that there was nothing wrong with her heart and lungs, nothing much wrong with her at all. Then why had she sometimes felt so ill that Jonathan had sent her to this horrible place?

"Are you sure you'll be all right, Mrs. Langford?"

She was at the door now, but young Mrs. Merry had got there first and was holding her by the arm.

Don't you dare touch me, you sneaking little bitch! were the words that formed in Amy's mind. It was appalling. She had never had such thoughts and feelings before.

"I think I'll be better alone," she said aloud, very faintly.

Sue Merry, still looking anxious, let her go. As Amy left the room she had a vision of all the rest of them at the table, looking after her with various degrees of concern on their faces, even Miss Pick. Bob Merry and Dr. Cunningham had actually got to their feet. There was no doubt that she was the centre of attention, was uppermost in all their minds.

It ought to have made her feel better, but it didn't help one little bit. As she crept up the wide staircase she wondered why it didn't help. The answer came with a sudden flash of insight as she entered the loneliness of her apartment. It didn't help because they would have behaved in exactly the same way if it had been anybody else who had felt ill and been obliged to leave the table.

Suppose it had been the crippled and twisted Mrs. Graham. With her dreadful new insight Amy saw that they would have been even more anxious and concerned.

She sat down on her bed and tried to still the rage and horror of her thoughts. It was so bitterly unfair. Obviously the others didn't understand. They had never been used to coming first, to being someone's very precious treasure, and what you had never had you did not miss. But she had had it all her life until these last nightmarish months, and how could she possibly live without it now?

It was all Jonathan's fault. He should have taken over where his father left off. Why, Philip had actually promised her that Jonathan would.

"Jonathan will take care of you," he had said one of the last times she saw him in the hospital, before the ward sister had suggested that it might perhaps be better if she did not come, because the sight of him struggling for breath distressed her so much.

It was a promise. She felt sure that Philip had spoken to Jonathan and that he had promised his father to look after her. Instead of which . . .

Amy felt herself gasping for breath. Every time she thought of that terrible scene it became even more vivid in her memory. She fell back against the cushions and stared without seeing at the beautiful ceiling mouldings that Mrs.

Graham so much admired. All around her was a deep blackness. Blackness and pain. How was it possible that she should suffer like this? It must not be allowed. Somebody must come and stop it at once. As they stopped it in the hospital when Jonathan was born; as they stopped it when she had the operation. As the doctor had stopped it with an injection when Jonathan had phoned him after they had that terrible scene.

Somebody must come and stop it. Amy must not be allowed to suffer in this way.

Time passed. The telephone on the bedside table rang. Automatically Amy stretched out a hand to lift the receiver.

"I do hope I'm not disturbing you, Mrs. Langford," said a female voice. "It's Sue Merry here. I just wondered if you were feeling better now, or whether there's anything we can do for you."

"I am much better, thank you," said Amy coolly, "and I am just about to go to sleep."

"I'm so glad. I won't ring again then, but will leave you to get in touch if you need me."

Amy put down the receiver. Interfering little whippersnapper, she cried aloud to herself.

It was surprising how much better she felt after saying this. She repeated it again aloud, and other phrases too, using the sort of words she would never have dreamed of using before she came to Digby Hall, words that she would have been appalled to hear on another's lips.

After a while she got up from the divan and sat in front of the dressing table, looking at herself in the mirror. As far as she could see, she looked just the same as ever. Grey hair very well cut and waved and with only the faintest of blue rinses. Blue eyes that had kept their colour and did not need much makeup. A fair complexion that she had taken great care of over the years.

She smiled at herself. That was better. There was nothing wrong with the image in the mirror. It was a charming image, pretty as a picture, as her father always used to say. Whatever would he think now, to see her so neglected and

ill-treated. He would be very angry. We must put a stop to
this at once, he would say. And he would do it too.

"Filthy little bitch, that warden," said Amy aloud to the
pretty picture in the mirror. "I'd like to wring her neck."

It fascinated her that the image could smile and look so
charming even while the lips formed such words. She
experimented further.

"The silly simpering old cow," she said, calling to mind
the crippled Mrs. Graham. "What's she got to live for?
Wouldn't take much to dispose of that little bundle of old
rags."

The blue eyes sparkled back at her; the pink lips settled
back into their cupid's bow as soon as they had finished
speaking. She leant forward and pressed her lips to the
image in the glass.

"Don't worry, Amy," she murmured. "You've not been
completely deserted. I'm going to look after you. I'm going
to make sure that you get your due and that those who won't
give it you will suffer for it."

She drew back again, smiled into the mirror, and patted
her hair.

"That's a promise, Amy," she said.

2

Oddly enough, the person from whom Amy had expected least of all proved to be the most congenial to her. She had been at Digby Hall for well over a week before she had any conversation with Mrs. Ramsden. After the bewilderment and despair of the first few days and the amazing discovery that relief lay within her own power, Amy had withdrawn as far as possible from contact with the other residents.

In the mornings she lay long in bed, dreaming of her former life. Then she got up and listened at the door of her apartment to make sure there was nobody on the landing and on the stairs before she came out. With luck she might then get off the premises unnoticed, or with no need to say more than a quick "Good morning," barely pausing in her walk as if she was in a hurry and had something very important to do. But once she had come out of the little cul-de-sac that led to Digby Hall and was on the broad suburban road that stretched away into the distance, leafy and deserted save for an occasional car going by, Amy's quick step faltered.

Where was she going? What was she going to do until lunchtime? It was no use shaking off Digby Hall and all its

19

hateful inhabitants if there was nothing better to put in their place. Now if she were to be called for in a car like Mrs. Ramsden . . .

Jonathan ought to be here, calling for her in a car, instead of gadding about in Holland or Rome or wherever he was. Amy stood still at the bus stop. At least it was better to look as if she was waiting for a bus rather than to be seen aimlessly stumbling along. Perhaps it might help to think and say aloud about Jonathan the sort of things she had been saying about the people at Digby Hall.

She tried but it didn't help. The memory of that scene with him returned in all its horror and she could no longer bear to stand still.

Nor could she endure to be alone. Far better to be back in her apartment, revelling in the comfort of her hatred for those in the other rooms, than out here in this leafy desert. To avoid going straight back she decided to go to the row of shops, in a side street a few yards away. There was nothing that she urgently needed, either for her own personal use or for the breakfast and light supper that the residents prepared for themselves. In any case, there was always food available on the premises, as well as household goods and some chemist's goods, for those who could not go out and shop for themselves.

Oh yes, everything had been thought of to keep you trapped, to stop you from writing to Jonathan and saying you couldn't possibly stay here because of so-and-so.

The woman in the greengrocer's remembered Amy from when she had come in on the first morning. There was nobody else in the shop and the woman was inclined to be chatty. She was a low-class sort of person, with lank black hair and a dirty overall.

"You're from Digby Hall, aren't you?" she said as she weighed the apples that Amy was probably going to throw into the bushes when she got back because she already had more than she wanted. "Lovely place, by all accounts. Wish I could afford to live there."

Amy handed over the money without deigning to reply. She would certainly never come into this shop again, but get any fruit or vegetables that she needed in the little supermarket. In the chemist's she lingered a long time selecting a toothbrush that she did not want. There were several other customers in the shop and the girl behind the counter was one of those dopey types who wouldn't remember you from one minute to the next.

Amy found it soothing to stand among the showcases of cosmetics and soap and bath essences. She was to spend a lot of time in that chemist's shop in the days to come.

The post office, too, was quite busy. By taking a long time to choose some writing paper, also not needed, and then waiting in a queue for stamps, Amy managed to kill more minutes. In the afternoons she remained in her apartment or sat alone on the seat under the lilac bushes, sometimes daydreaming, sometimes thinking the thoughts of hatred and violence that both comforted and frightened her. Evenings could be drugged with television. At the communal meal she ate modestly but adequately and only spoke if somebody spoke to her first.

Nobody seemed to notice that there was anything different about her at all.

"The fools," she said to the image in the mirror every night when she renewed her promise to look after Amy and punish those who made her suffer. "Just you wait, you fools."

But sometimes the time of waiting seemed very long.

One morning she decided to go and visit her former neighbours. It meant a bus ride into the centre of town, then changing onto a bus going in a different direction.

"I shall not be in to lunch today," she said to Mrs. Merry in the aloof manner of the mistress of the house giving instructions to her maid.

The silly little creature actually smiled at her. What right had she to smile or not? She was just there to receive instructions. Worse than that. She actually spoke.

"I hope you will have a pleasant day, Mrs. Langford."

"Thank you," said Amy even more aloofly than before.

The thought of stripping that smile off that silly little face lasted Amy happily to the bus stop and for most of the ride into town. On the way out to her old home Amy was not so happy. The familiar streets brought back memories, and the terrible truth that she had been denying to herself as well as telling lies to others: the beautiful bungalow with the sun lounge that overlooked the sea was not hers to return to if she could find a suitable housekeeper-companion.

It had been sold. There would be strangers there.

Jonathan had spared her all the details. In that way, at least, he had carried out his father's promise to her. She had been housed at his flat in London during the last week before she moved to Digby Hall, and both he and his daily woman had been very considerate to her. In some ways it had been quite a happy week, but it had come to an end, and now Jonathan was gadding about again, and Amy was getting off the bus at the terminus, right up at the top of the hill.

It always had been a windy place, and even on this balmy June morning the breeze disordered her hair. Everything looked at the same time very familiar and very strange. The hotel at the crossroads, the garage where Philip took the car to be serviced, the shopping parade where they all knew Amy and treated her with proper respect. That was just as it had always been. They had been good customers at the local shops, she and Philip, and would not be quickly forgotten. As she walked along the wide pavement of the shopping parade Amy had an impulse to go into one or two of the shops. There was no need to buy anything. They would recognise her and treat her with deference, as they always had done, keeping other people waiting in order to speak to her.

"What a great pleasure to see you, Mrs. Langford!"

"We do miss you—it hasn't been the same since you left."

Oh yes, Amy felt sure that she could rely on the shopkeepers. But they would also ask questions. "How is your son?" And, "How do you like your new home?"

The pleasure of the greetings would be ruined by the pain of the questions. Amy decided to pass by without stopping.

The bungalow was only five minutes' walk away. When

she caught sight of it Amy suddenly stood still. Whatever
had come over her? Something seemed to have slipped in
her mind and for a minute or two she had really believed
that she was going home. But the bungalow was no longer
home; there would be strangers there now, and she was
going to call on Mr. and Mrs. Farquharson, who had been
their neighbours for fifteen years. Or rather on Mrs.
Farquharson, because Mr. Farquharson would be at his
office. He was ten years younger than Philip.

But would Marjorie Farquharson be there? Amy was so
confused that it took her several minutes to remember what
day it was. Thursday. Didn't Marjorie go somewhere on
Thusdays? Charity shop, or something like that? And on
some other days too. Amy's thoughts fell into place and she
remembered that she had often felt irritated with Marjorie
because she always seemed to be rushing about to this, that,
and the other just when Amy wanted her to come in for a
cup of coffee and a chat.

It seemed only too likely that Marjorie would be rushing
off somewhere now. Yes, the car was gone. Arnold always
left it in the drive for her before he went to work because
Marjorie found it difficult to manage the awkward turn out
of the garage. So she would be out somewhere and would
probably remain out for hours, never dreaming, of course,
that Amy might be calling and badly wanting to talk to her.
But then, Marjorie always had been rather a selfish woman.
Very fond of all her good works but forgetting that charity
begins at home.

A ring at the bell confirmed Amy's assumption that there
was nobody in. She leant against the side of the porch to
steady herself. The sun was very hot and she felt weak and
dizzy, not at all fit to be paying calls, but longing for
somewhere to sit down and for a cup of coffee and a friendly
voice. Perhaps it would be best to go back to the shopping
parade. The baker's shop had a few chairs and tables and
served light refreshments, but it was rather crowded and
noisy, and she might be greeted by acquaintances who
would ask questions.

The hotel might be better. It was not much used by local

people during the day, and she could probably sit quietly in the lounge for a while.

On the other hand, Amy had never been into a hotel by herself. Suddenly it struck her as quite outrageous that she should ever have to think of going into a hotel by herself. Why on earth was not Marjorie Farquharson at home? Or if she was not at home, why on earth was she not driving over to Digby Hall to collect Amy to go for a drive or back to her own place for the day? If Amy could make the journey on the bus, why couldn't Marjorie do it in her own car?

It was no distance at all. It was horribly unkind not to have come to take Amy out before now. Yet again anger acted as a therapy. As she stood thinking that she had never really liked Marjorie very much, in spite of their being neighbours for so long, Amy found her dizziness going and her limbs growing stronger. She would go back to the baker's, she decided; have a chat with Mrs. George and let herself be persuaded to stop for a cup of tea and one of those delicious Danish pastries. Mrs. George was a great gossip. If Amy directed the conversation carefully she might even hear something to Marjorie's disadvantage. It was worth trying. It would give her an immediate aim, an incentive to move away from the Farquharsons' front door.

She walked firmly back to the gate and then began to feel rather weak again and stood hesitating, wondering whether, after all, she could face the hot and noisy baker's shop.

"Why, it's Mrs. Langford," said a woman's voice. "I didn't expect to see you here."

Amy didn't know whether to be glad or sorry at the encounter. It was Mrs. Court, the neighbour on the other side whose husband always pretended to be deafer than he really was. She was an insignificant little woman and not much to talk to either, being sloppy and untidy about the house and never seeming to know anything of what was going on in the neighbourhood. Marjorie said that she was very clever and helped Mr. Court write his history books, but Amy found that very hard to believe.

"Hullo, Mrs. Court," she said weakly. They had never

been on Christian-name terms. "I came to visit Mrs. Farquharson," she went on, "but I think there must be some misunderstanding. There's nobody at home."

This would give the impression that it had been a firm arrangement. In fact, it would have been much more sensible to have telephoned before coming; Amy realised that now.

"Oh dear," said Mrs. Court. "I don't suppose they got a message to you in time. What a pity that you should have had a journey for nothing. Mrs. Farquharson is in hospital."

"Good heavens!" Amy was shocked. Whatever next? Was there no end to the shocks she was to receive?

"Yesterday morning," said Mrs. Court. "She was taken ill very suddenly, fortunately before her husband had left for work. It was a heart attack."

"But, but . . ." Amy had been going to say, But it's impossible, she's tough as old boots. Fortunately she stopped herself before the words actually came out.

"Yes, I know," said Mrs. Court sympathetically. "It's a dreadful shock. Why, it's made you quite pale, Mrs. Langford. Come in and have some tea. Or brandy or something."

Amy accepted. She really did feel that if she didn't sit down soon she would probably fall down. And whatever the deficiencies of Mrs. Court's person and household, there was one big thing to be said for her in the present situation: she was totally without curiosity and would not ask any questions about where Amy was living now and how she liked it.

"I'm so sorry," said Amy when she was seated in Mrs. Court's untidy living room, with books and papers all over the place, and the torn chairs and settee where the cat had been scratching. "I'm so sorry to be so silly, but it really was a shock. Yes, tea, please. It's very kind of you."

I hope the cups will be clean, she said to herself when Mrs. Cort had gone into the kitchen. Marjorie Farquharson having a heart attack. It was really quite incredible. But it served her right for rushing about so much. What an age the woman was being with the tea! And how ghastly the room looked. There was one good thing, though. Amy had been so taken aback by this news and by Mrs. Court's invitation to come in that she had walked past her own former home without thinking about it, barely noticing it, in fact.

"What do they say at the hospital?" asked Amy when Mrs. Court came back with a tray. The cups looked clean enough and there were some digestive biscuits, not Amy's favourite but better than nothing. It was getting on for lunchtime and she was beginning to feel hungry as well as upset.

"I believe she was beginning to improve last night," said Mrs. Court. "I don't know the latest news, but Peter and I are going round this evening to see if she is allowed any visitors."

It occurred to Amy for the first time that perhaps she ought to visit her former neighbour, or at any rate look as if she intended to.

"What should one take?" she asked. "I expect she'll be flooded with flowers . . . is she allowed to eat anything? What do you think, Mrs. Court?"

"Oh," said Mrs. Court in her breathless way, "I'm so sorry. I didn't make it plain. I meant we would be going round to Mr. Farquharson to ask him whether she would want us to go to the hospital. I didn't mean we would be visiting Mrs. Farquharson herself this evening. I believe she is in the intensive-care unit."

"I see," said Amy. What a relief, she added to herself. "Then I'd better just send a card," she said aloud, "and phone the hospital before I go and see her."

"I think that really would be best," agreed Mrs. Court.

Amy ate another biscuit, accepted another cup of tea, thanked Mrs. Court and said she really would have to be going. Not a word had been said that did not relate to Marjorie Farquharson's illness, no reference was made to Amy's move from the area, and it never occurred to Amy to ask after Mr. Court or Mrs. Court's own state of health.

She said good-bye to Mrs. Court with the thought that she did not care in the least if she never saw her again, walked past her own former home once more without even glancing

at it, along the parade of shops without feeling any impulse
to go into any of them, and got onto the bus that was waiting
at the terminus.

The whole of her former life seemed quite unreal, as
insubstantial as a dream. The only thing that seemed to be
of any relevance to Amy Langford at all was that somebody
as young as Marjorie Farquharson, as active and energetic,
could actually have a serious heart attack, could perhaps
even die. In one way it was frightening, in another it was
exhilarating. If Marjorie Farquharson could die, then others
older than she and less robust could also die.

Death.

Death meant the breath leaving the body. If it was a
feeble body and a frail breath it would not take much to
expel it forever. Amy thought about this all the way back in
the bus. It fascinated her. The journey seemed to go by in no
time.

Mrs. Ramsden, of the dyed hair and the raucous laugh,
got off the bus at the nearest stop for Digby Hall. Amy had
not noticed her get on, and it was actually Mrs. Ramsden
who was the first to speak as they walked along together.

"Can't say I usually feel glad to be getting back to the
institution, but I've had such a frustrating morning that I'm
past caring."

"I've had a rotten morning too," said Amy.

Mrs. Ramsden made some sort of a grunt in reply and
they walked for a moment or two in silence side by side,
each contemplating the rottenness of her morning, with no
friendly feelings towards the other but without any ill will
either, rather like two tramlines running in parallel.

Amy found it strangely restful to walk alongside the
disgruntled Mrs. Ramsden. No sort of effort of any kind
was required, and for some reason or other Mrs. Ramsden
did not arouse in her those intense feelings of hatred and
fury that half delighted and half frightened her. She even
felt that she could tell Mrs. Ramsden about what she had
been thinking—how easily the breath could leave a frail
body—without Mrs. Ramsden being shocked or surprised.

When they got back to Digby Hall she asked Mrs.
Ramsden if she would like to come up to her apartment with
her and have something to eat. It was the first time she had
invited any of the other residents into her own quarters.
Mrs. Ramsden accepted.

"A cheese sandwich?" suggested Amy. "Or would you
rather have something cooked?"

It was said in the most offhand and unceremonious
manner. The Mrs. Langford who had presided over the
hospitality offered at the beautiful architect-designed bungalow would never have dreamed of speaking in such a
way.

"Cheese sandwich," said Mrs. Ramsden collapsing into
an armchair. "Why go to any more trouble? Thanks a lot."
She yawned and then gave her ugly laugh. "God—isn't it
wonderful not to have to be polite!"

That was the moment when the little light by which Amy
Langford had always tried to lead her life flickered and went
out forever. She did not feel it as a light going out but more
as a release. There was no sense of shock at Mrs.
Ramsden's remark. Politeness no longer seemed to matter.
Amy expected nothing of Mrs. Ramsden and did not care
what Mrs. Ramsden thought of her. They drank their coffee
and ate their sandwiches almost in silence. Amy thought of
asking about Mrs. Ramsden's frustrating morning but
decided against it. She was not the least bit interested in
Mrs. Ramsden's troubles, nor had she any desire to tell Mrs.
Ramsden about her own.

It was very strange. With anybody else she would have
been bitterly offended by now because they had not made
sympathetic enquiries. It was almost as if Mrs. Ramsden
was not another human being at all but a part of herself. All
that she needed to do to get on with Mrs. Ramsden was to
consult this part of herself.

"Don't you like the meals in the dining room?" Amy
knew that this was the right thing to say.

"Food's all right," was the brusque reply. "It's the
company."

Amy experienced a little shiver of delighted anticipation. What luck that she and Mrs. Ramsden had met privately, so to speak, and not tried to talk to each other in public, for if that had been the case they would never have reached such a quick and full understanding. Here at last was something to look forward to and fill the blankness of her days until the time came when she could carry out the nightly promise that she made to herself when she looked with love and admiration at the image in the mirror.

"Which of them do you like best?" she asked.

It might be as well to let Mrs. Ramsden take the lead. After all, Amy herself did not particularly mind what order the inhabitants of Digby Hall were placed in for the picking over. The main thing was to have somebody with whom to play the game. Disagreement on points of detail was unimportant. Indeed, it might even add to the joys of the conversation.

Mrs. Ramsden laughed. the sound was ugly but it no longer grated on Amy.

"Hadn't you better ask, Mrs. Langford, which of them do I find least intolerable?"

"All right then. Which of them do you find least intolerable?"

"That's easy. Clement Horder."

"Why?" Amy was a little surprised. She would probably, herself, have put Mr. Horder at the other end of the scale, because it was in connection with him that she had suffered her greatest disappointment.

"Because you don't have to talk to him," said Mrs. Ramsden with a loud guffaw.

"And he's not bad to look at, which is more than can be said for Dr. Cummingham. I hate fat men, don't you?"

"In general yes, I do. Although my husband was definitely on the large side. That's what killed him, poor old chap. Too much of everything."

Mrs. Ramsden's broad face took on quite a sentimental expression. In Amy's opinion it did not suit her, and in any case it was not playing the game. Sentiment and sympathy had no place in her unspoken pact with Mrs. Ramsden, and she made no response.

Either Amy's silence or the expression on her face recalled the other woman to the business in hand.

"You don't want to trust George Cunningham," she said.

Trust! As if Amy would trust any of them, least of all Mrs. Ramsden herself. She began to think that the woman must be rather stupid, but that didn't matter. In fact, it might almost be turned to Amy's advantage. If she was going to carry out her promise to herself, she would need an accomplice—somebody to find things out and to do things that it would be better for Amy not to do herself. And if the accomplice was too stupid to realise that she was being used and manipulated, that would make it all much safer for Amy.

"You don't mean Dr. Cunningham is a fraud—not a real doctor at all!" said Amy with a little schoolgirlish giggle that she knew would both appeal to Mrs. Ramsden and help to throw dust in her eyes about Amy's true intentions.

"Oh yes, he's qualified all right," was the reply. "I looked him up in the directory. My husband and I were in the same line of business, you might say." Pause for a laugh. "We ran a private nursing home."

"Did you really? How very interesting."

"It was bloody hard work. That's one thing I do have to say about that scruffy young couple. They're workers all right."

"You mean Mr. and Mrs. Merry?"

"That's right. Sue's a good cook and she's always cleaning, and Bob's doing some sort of part-time training course to qualify himself."

"They seem to me very young to be in charge," ventured Amy.

"Oh, my dear, they're not in charge. They are only employees, doing the daily chores. Anything that really matters is decided by the Committee."

Amy made further enquiries, saying she did not know the details of how Digby Hall was run, because she had been in a state of shock after her husband's death and her son had arranged everything for her. Mrs. Ramsden seemed very

pleased to hold forth, and Amy listened in the same way as
she had once listened to Philip, picking out with unerring
instinct those things that were of interest and importance to
her and letting all the rest drift by unheard.

The Committee was composed mainly of local worthies
and met in the late afternoon of the first Thursday of every
month in the dining room at Digby Hall. Finances were
competently looked after by a firm of accountants, and Amy
gathered that there were only two people who really
mattered. One was the Hon. Secretary, a retired civil
servant called Ernest Fisher, whom Mrs. Ramsden described as a "dried-up little fusspot"; and the other was
Mrs. Gurney, who had been chosen, or who had selected
herself, to act as "Visitor to the Residents," ostensibly to
hear any complaints and report them to the Committee, but
really, so Mrs. Ramsden said and Amy could well believe
it, to enjoy herself poking her nose into other people's
affairs.

"Always turns up at the most inconvenient moment,"
grumbled Mrs. Ramsden, "when you're setting your hair or
have just settled down for a nice bit of shut-eye. Stands
there at the door dripping with jewellery and all sweet and
simpering. 'Oh, I'm so sorry. Did I disturb you? I just
wondered if everything was all right.' Yuk."

"Patronising," said Amy, feeling that she had been given
a very clear picture of Mrs. Gurney.

"You've said it. Likes to feel she's going slumming
among the poor old has-beens at the workhouse. Lady
Bloody Bountiful. You'd think with the rents we have to
pay here we'd be free from that sort of thing."

From sheer habit Amy was about to say that she didn't
know what the rents were, since her son dealt with all that
for her, but she caught herself up in time. It was quite
inappropriate to be helpless little Amy when she was with
Mrs. Ramsden, although there might be other circumstances in which the character could usefully be assumed.

It was strange how these last days had changed her. She
had always known, she supposed, but she had never before
been conscious of using it as a weapon. She had believed

herself to be fragile Amy and was very frightened of being bumped or bruised. But now she seemed to have become two people. Fragile Amy was the charming image in the mirror who had to be loved and protected at all costs. The other Amy was the one who looked at her and promised her revenge on all those who had distressed fragile Amy. The other Amy was not helpless at all. She was very strong and cunning. She could make mincemeat of the vulgar and garrulous Mrs. Ramsden.

"Tell me more about Mrs. Gurney," she said.

Mrs. Ramsden told her. The Lady Visitor had apparently interrupted Mrs. Ramsden when she was having her glass of sherry one evening and had tried to tell her that solitary consumption of alcohol by the residents was frowned on by the Committee.

"But there's no such rule," said Amy.

"Of course there's no such rule. If there were, her boyfriend George Cunningham would be breaking it all the time."

Amy pricked up her ears. "Dr. Cunningham?"

"Thick as thieves. Or rather, she'd like to be, but he's a bit wary in spite of all her money and her luxury villa. You can't trust him, though. Everything you say goes straight to Madame Gurney."

"I see." Amy was thoughtful. Then she smiled. "Miss Pick hasn't a hope, then."

"Nancy Pick?" Out came the guffaw. "Oh, she's not in the running. I don't think she's seriously trying. Although one never knows." It was Mrs. Ramsden's turn to look thoughtful. "I wouldn't put it past George to do a bit of gossiping over the chessboard."

"Chess?"

"Yes, didn't you know? Twice a week—regular as clockwork. Mondays in Dr. Cunningham's flat, Fridays in Nancy's. It's chess from half-past eight till eleven o'clock."

Amy felt she had to believe this. Had it been any other woman she would have suspected that the chess was an alibi for a very different sort of relationship, but not with the horse-like Miss Pick. Presumably she had some sort of cleverness.

"She used to teach science," said Mrs. Ramsden. "Can't you just see her crashing about the lab?"

"And now it looks as if she's trying to be teacher's pet running around after the Merrys all the time."

"Oh, she gets a reduction in rent for helping in the house. She'd never be able to afford it otherwise."

"I see. That's interesting," said Amy.

"If you really want a teacher's pet, there's Mrs. Graham. She's the blue-eyed girl who can do no wrong. You'd think nobody had ever had arthritis before, the way Sue Merry fusses over her. You or I could be dying before we got half so much attention."

"But Mrs. Graham really is very crippled," said Amy with the air of somebody trying to be reasonable and fair.

Mrs. Ramsden made a grimace. "I know. It's a horrible complaint. Haven't I nursed plenty of them? Of course she needs help, poor old thing. Nobody denies that. But I do wish she'd lose her temper sometimes or at least get a bit tetchy. It's all this bloody sweetness and patience. I know it's very wrong of me but I can't help it. She gets my goat."

"Mine too."

They laughed together. "Aren't we awful," said Amy in the schoolgirlish manner that she knew instinctively was the right line to take with Mrs. Ramsden.

"And isn't it doing us good," said the latter. "I feel miles better than I did when I came in."

"So do I. Oh, do you have to go now?"

Mrs. Ramsden had got to her feet. "I think I'd better. I changed Mr. Horder's library books for him when I was in town and he'll be wanting them. He reads a lot."

"It must be a great comfort to him," said Amy, following Mrs. Ramsden into the more charitable and mellow mood into which she seemed to have talked herself. It looked as if Mrs. Ramsden was rather subject to moods. When feeling tired and frustrated and irritable she would enjoy malicious gossip, but one could not rely on her for any steadiness of purpose. As soon as she felt rested and contented she would go all soft and sentimental. Mrs. Ramsden's moods would have to be watched very carefully.

"What did Mr. Horder do before he retired?" she asked as they moved toward the door of the apartment.

"I think he was an accountant, but he's crazy about wildlife. Particularly plants. He goes for long walks on the downs looking for rare specimens. I've got him some botany books he wanted. It's about the only thing that went right for me this morning."

Amy felt that she ought to ask what it was that had gone wrong, but it was silly to start an entirely fresh conversation standing there at the door. Besides, she had had enough of Mrs. Ramsden. As a fellow rebel and an informant about all matters to do with Digby Hall she was good company, but if she was going to talk about her former life and her activities outside the house, then she would become a bore.

The Amy Langford of ten days ago would have been willing to listen, or rather to pretend to listen, in exchange for the chance to talk about herself to a seemingly interested hearer. The Amy Langford of today no longer had any desire to strike such an unspoken bargain, for she had quite different aims in view.

"You just come again," she said aloud. "Early one evening. Cocktail time. We'll drink whatever we like, and if Mrs. Gurney decides to interfere we'll just ask her to join the party."

This went down well. She likes her drink, thought Amy as she closed the door behind her visitor. And she's also a bit sweet on Mr. Horder, for all that pretence of hating everybody in the place. Fancy running around getting his library books! As if he couldn't go and get them for himself. Being deaf wouldn't stop him from going to the library. Silly fool of a woman! That wasn't the way to gain power over a man, by running around catering to his every whim. Amy could have told her, but she was not going to tell her, because Mrs. Ramsden's weak spot about Mr. Horder might well come in useful one of these days.

All the odd bits of information might come in useful. Amy thought them over and filed them away in her mind as she carried the tray to the kitchen and did the little bit of washing-up straightaway. She was tidy by nature and always disliked seeing anything undone that ought to be done. This too could be an important asset in her big enterprise.

When she had cleaned up in the kitchen she walked over to the mirror that hung over the dressing table in the big room and stared lovingly at her image. There were still several hours to go before the time when she usually renewed her promise, but the talk with Mrs. Ramsden had greatly stimulated and encouraged her. It seemed unkind not to let the sweet and charming Amy know at once that plans for revenge were taking shape. Besides, she felt very exciting and was bursting to talk about it.

"I'm beginning to get an idea how to set about it," she said to the pretty smiling face in the mirror. "I'm afraid I may not be able to take them in the order you want me to. It will have to be as the opportunity arises. But nobody will be left out, I promise you that."

She smiled at the face, kissed it, and then went and lay on the divan bed, propped herself against the cushions, and stared out of the window. It was a big window, taking up much of that side of the room, and next to it was the long window that opened on to the tiny balcony. The balcony was divided into two by a low partition, half of it belonging to Amy's apartment, and half to the apartment next door, which was occupied by Dr. Cunningham. A very convenient arrangement for romantic assignations, but there might also be other encounters for which it would be very convenient. Presumably Dr. Cunningham kept the long window bolted, as Amy did herself, and used the other window when he wanted air.

Two of Amy's casements were open now. The air was mild and fragrant. In the ground-floor apartment underneath Amy's, Mrs. Graham breathed in the garden scents with pleasure as she took her afternoon rest. Amy was aware of nothing outside her own thoughts.

The view from this side of the house was of a slope of beech trees, now brightly shimmering in their early-summer green under the afternoon sun. The woman who had lived in the apartment before Amy had loved that view. She had been a great traveller, and it had comforted her and given her a sense of freedom from the constraints of old age and weakness when she lay and looked at the beech trees against the sky.

Amy Langford did not even see the trees. Her eyes were turned inwards, examining her mental filing system. Mr. Horder's deafness and Mrs. Ramsden's weakness for him and for alcoholic drinks; Mrs. Graham's physical frailty and Sue Merry's fussing; Miss Pick and the Lady Visitor Mrs. Gurney as rivals for Dr. George Cunningham's attentions; the twice-weekly game of chess; Mr. Ernest Fisher, the tiresome bureaucrat of an Hon. Secretary—no doubt he would be a thorn in the flesh of the young Merrys, who were only employees and not in charge.

There was promise in all these factors and in many others, still unknown, but which Amy proposed to find out about either on her own or through Mrs. Ramsden.

Amy withdrew her eyes from the middle distance outside the window and glanced down at her hands, resting lightly folded against the blue summer frock. They were delicate, well-shaped hands, competent enough in their own way, but ready at any time to give an appearance of fluttering helplessness. What pretty hands they were! How different from Miss Pick's rough, uncared-for claws, from the feeble twisted fingers of Mrs. Graham, or the broad, ugly, overjewelled hands of Mrs. Ramsden.

Such pretty hands. And such a clever mind to direct them.

"Clever Amy," she said aloud, then raised each hand in turn to her lips and kissed it tenderly. "Clever Amy."

3

"I have been wondering," said Mrs. Graham to Mrs. Merry a couple of weeks later, "whether there is any chance of my moving into another flat. It's not that I haven't been very happy in this one. You know I have, but the fact is . . ."

Her voice faded away. Sue Merry looked at her with some anxiety. It was half-past nine in the evening, a hot and sultry summer evening, but Mrs. Graham had asked to have the windows shut and the curtains drawn across instead of lying there, as had been her custom, enjoying the last scents of the garden and the last light in the sky.

Sue was puzzled as well as anxious. Mrs. Graham's condition was deteriorating, of course, as it was bound to do with the passage of time. She had angina as well as severe arthritis. But Dr. Mercer, who had been called in to see her several times lately, could not find any particular cause for alarm. It almost looked as if Mrs. Graham's attacks were being caused by her own fears, which was very odd, because she was not in general a nervous person and had always been reluctant to cause any trouble and have the doctor sent for.

37

Something was worrying Mrs. Graham badly, and Sue was determined to try to find out what it was.

"I'm sure we'll be able to find someone to change flats with you if you really want to," she said reassuringly. "It'll have to go before the Committee, of course, but we've got a week before the next meeting, so there'll be time for us to sound people out to see if anyone would be willing to swap. But perhaps we can put things right without your having to move out. You've always seemed to like this flat. No stairs to climb and just a little way to the dining room and the sun terrace and the garden."

"Oh yes, indeed!" cried Mrs. Graham with a renewal of energy. "It's been lovely."

"But it isn't any longer?" Sue cocked her head on one side and smiled her lopsided smile.

What an attractive little thing she is, thought Mrs. Graham. Sensible and practical too. And very warmhearted and understanding. Surely it would be possible to tell her the truth without getting Mrs. Langford into difficulties. Surely Sue Merry would understand. On the other hand, Sue might think it her duty to pass it on to the Committee, and in any case, Mrs. Graham had given her promise to Mrs. Langford, and a promise was a sacred thing.

"It's still lovely," she said to Sue, "but the fact is that now I'm becoming such a very feeble old thing I'm beginning to feel rather isolated down here in the evening and at night."

"I see." Sue became thoughtful. This was a perfectly reasonable objection on the part of Mrs. Graham. The apartment was next to the dining room, and there was nobody else living on the ground floor at this side of the house. Beyond the dining room were the kitchen and utility rooms, not used evenings and nights, and the other side of the wide entrance hall, which also served as a lounge, was the only other resident's flat on the ground floor. Its occupant was the deaf Mr. Horder.

On the first floor lived Mrs. Langford, Dr. Cunningham, Mrs. Ramsden, and the Merrys themselves, and on the attic floor above were the guest rooms for the use of residents' friends, and the small flat occupied by Miss Pick.

Mrs. Graham's flat was rather cut off from the others, but up till now she had not seemed to mind at all.

"You've only got to phone and I'll be down with you in no time," said Sue. "Any time of the night. The phone rings by my bed."

"I know, my dear."

Mrs. Graham's fingers moved over the bedspread. Her voice sounded faint again. She really was a very frail old lady, and rather more of a responsibility than Sue had expected to have when she and Bob undertook to provide one main meal a day, look after the maintenance of the building and gardens, and send for a doctor if any of the residents became ill. They had taken the job primarily because it gave them a home and was convenient for Bob to get on with his studies, but both of them liked old people, and they were conscientious and hardworking. They were always very conscious, however, that neither of them had any nursing qualifications or experience. Some members of the Committee, including the careful Mr. Ernest Fisher, had been against their appointment for this reason. But the majority, led by the formidable Mrs. Gurney, had argued that the young couple, for this very reason, could be got on the cheap, and this argument had carried the day. Mrs. Gurney, like so many rich people, was very fond of saving money in small ways, whether it was her own money or somebody else's.

Besides, the youth and inexperience of the Merrys gave her an excellent excuse for even more visits to Digby Hall.

Sue Merry had been worried about Mrs. Graham from the first, and dreaded that she might become too weak to look after herself. When such a thing happened, residents were supposed to make their own arrangements to be nursed or to take themselves elsewhere. Mrs. Graham had no near relatives and she loved Digby Hall. Sue was determined that she should not be bundled off into hospital if it could possibly be avoided.

"Would you really feel happier in one of the first-floor flats?" she asked gently.

"I think I would," was the faint reply.

"And you wouldn't mind the stairs?"

"They are nice easy stairs," said Mrs. Graham rather more strongly. "And in any case, if I didn't feel like coming down to lunch I could always make something for myself in my flat. I'm not as feeble as all that."

But she was feeble as all that. Sue could see Mrs. Graham starving herself. Unless she, Sue Merry, took to running up and down with trays of food, which was much frowned upon, both by the Committee and by the other residents. Sue had already been told off by Mrs. Gurney for taking Mr. Horder some supper when he had a bad feverish cold. On that occasion Sue and Bob had stood up for themselves when summoned before the Committee, and the general opinion had been that it was a very venial offence. They were to use their discretion in performing little services for the residents, but on no account were they ever to take on long-term nursing and care.

The rule made sense. Suppose all six residents were to become bedridden. Sue and Bob could not possibly cope, even if they had known how to. They discussed the problem of Mrs. Graham together.

"I really do think she'd be happier upstairs," said Sue, "and we'll have to find some way of making sure she gets enough to eat."

Bob Merry agreed. "But who's going to swap flats with her?"

"Not Mrs. Ramsden. She's not going to put herself out for anybody."

"Mrs. Langford?"

"I don't know," said Sue slowly. "She seems to be friendly enough towards Mrs. Graham. I've often seen them chatting on the terrace. But it seems a bit mean to ask her to move when she hasn't been here very long. And besides—"

"You don't like her," interrupted Bob. "Neither do I."

"Why don't we like her?"

The young Merrys, relaxing in their sitting room after clearing up the midday meal, considered this question.

"She's too well preserved," said Sue.

"She's a spoilt old puss."

"I don't trust her. She's too sickly sweet."

"I bet her husband had a hell of a life."

"And her son must have had a flaming row to get her to come and live here."

"She's perfectly healthy. There's no reason why she shouldn't have kept on a home of her own."

"None at all," agreed Sue, "except that she'd be miserable without a husband or somebody else to nag at to do what she wanted all the time."

"Perhaps she's trying to acquire another husband," suggested Bob.

"It'll have to be Mr. Horder then. If she's trying for Dr. Cunningham, Madam Gurney will scratch her eyes out."

They both laughed. Then Bob said: "If Mrs. Gurney ever does get Dr. Cunningham to marry her I reckon she'll soon be found dead in her bath and he'll be a wealthy widower."

"You've been reading too many thrillers," said Sue. "Dr. Cunningham's all right. And we're wandering off the point. What are we going to do about getting Mrs. Graham up to a first-floor flat?"

"Sound out Dr. Cunningham himself. If he's willing to swap and make it seem as if the whole thing has come from him in the first place, then we'll have no trouble with Mrs. Gurney or the Committee."

Bob Merry was quite good at summing up other people. He had done a variety of temporary jobs since leaving school and had sometimes acted as a peacemaking force among his mates in factory or office. He had a good brain and plenty of practical skill, but before he married Sue he had tended to flit about and waste his talents. It was Sue who suggested the technology courses and encouraged Bob in his studies. He depended on her a lot but did not like it to be thought that he did so, and she felt the double burden of supporting him without letting it be seen that this was what she was doing.

But in minor matters Bob was a support to her. Whether she could rely on him in a crisis had not yet been tested.

Sounding out Dr. Cunningham, for whom in fact Bob had

a great respect, was just the sort of thing the young man
enjoyed, and in the course of a friendly chat about the
respective merits of the residents' apartments in Digby Hall,
he discovered that Dr. Cunningham had always rather
coveted the ground-floor flat occupied by Mrs. Graham. In
addition to the usual accommodation it boasted a small extra
room which the old lady did not use, but that Dr.
Cunningham, who had recently taken up photography,
thought might do as a darkroom.

"Of course I hope we shall have her with us a long time
yet," said Dr. Cunningham, "but it's got to be faced that
nature is going to take its course sooner or later, and if that
flat ever falls vacant, Bob, then you'll find me heading the
list of applicants. In fact, between you and me, young man,
I've already mentioned it to the Secretary."

But not to Mrs. Gurney, said Bob to himself. Bad luck,
Mrs. Gurney. You'll never shift George Cunningham out of
that ground-floor flat. And he's going to be in it rather
sooner than he thinks."

"Well, isn't that extraordinary," he said aloud. "Mrs.
Graham was only saying to Sue the other day that she
wished she was living on the first floor."

The changeover was accomplished with the minimum of
delay. Only Mrs. Gurney, perhaps scenting the defeat of her
hopes, resisted it, but after a long private conversation with
Dr. Cunningham, she was understood to have withdrawn
her objections.

"No doubt our George has his methods," remarked Bob
Merry to Sue.

On the evening of the day when Mrs. Graham was installed
in the flat next to Mrs. Langford on the first floor, Amy held
a particularly long conversation with the charming image in
the mirror.

"Oh, I am so clever, Amy," she murmured. "So very
clever. You just can't imagine. Nobody has the remotest
idea. Everybody thinks Mrs. Graham wanted to be moved.
They've not a notion that it's because of what I've been
telling her. And doing to her! Intruders stealing into the

grounds and trying to get in through her window! That really was fun that evening, Amy. A terrible risk, but great fun. She looked so bad that I really thought I'd done the job there and then. But I'm glad they pulled her round. It's more of a challenge this way. My goodness, how I've had them all running about! I'm longing to get this one over and on with the next one. It's almost too easy now. Another few days, then we'll finish it. No longer, just in case she lets something slip. But I'm sure she won't, because a promise is a promise to her, and she really was crying, the silly old cow, when I told her how afraid I was of being turned out of Digby Hall if people knew I had these lapses of memory and had got myself locked out one night and tried to get in through her window! Never nervous before, but that settled her.

"Oh Amy, my precious, I am so clever. I'm going to enjoy this so much .and I'm going to enjoy telling you . . ."

Sue Merry did not realize at first that Mrs. Graham was dead. The old lady was lying peacefully with her eyes closed and her face pressed against the pillow. The wispy grey hair was very untidy, but then it always was first thing in the morning. The hands were outside the bedclothes, which were disturbed as if she had been pushing them away. It had been a hot night and Sue herself had been throwing aside the blankets. It seemed a pity to wake Mrs. Graham, but on the other hand Sue knew that she would be glad to see her. The move upstairs hadn't helped very much up till now. The old lady still seemed very nervous and unhappy, clinging to Sue when she brought her tea as if she could not bear to let her go.

"Here you are, Mrs. Graham dear."

Sue put the tray on the bedside table. Five minutes later she called Bob and stood holding his hand and weeping silently. It was two and a half years since they had taken on the job at Digby Hall, and this was the first time that one of the people in their care had died. They had been particularly attached to Mrs. Graham and they felt it keenly.

"We must phone Dr. Mercer," said Bob.

"It seems awful just to leave her," muttered Sue.

"There's nothing you can do. And nobody can get in without our master key."

As he spoke, Bob Merry automatically glanced at the long window that opened onto the balcony and that was now closed and bolted. Sue picked up the tray. At the sight of the unused teacup her eyes filled with tears again. They came quietly out onto the first-floor landing. There was nobody about. It was not quite eight o'clock and none of the residents had yet emerged. Bob pulled the door of the apartment shut, and the listener behind the door of the neighbouring apartment heard the slight click of the latch. It had made a similar little click when she herself had come out six hours earlier, after accomplishing the task, and had given her a moment's anxiety. But all other doors had been shut, the house was quiet, and the only light to be seen was that left burning all night in the entrance lounge. She had slipped silently back into her own flat and bolted the window and put the polythene container back over the new blouse and replaced it in the drawer, and then she had whispered into the mirror for some time before getting into bed and instantly falling asleep.

"It could have happened anytime," said Dr. Mercer to the two young Merrys.

She was a pleasant-faced, plumpish, middle-aged woman, and Bob and Sue felt better after her arrival."

"You don't think we could have done anything to prevent it?" said Sue.

The doctor shook her head. "There was nothing anybody could have done."

But Sue still looked anxious. "I wonder if it was anything to do with the strain of moving into a different flat."

"It might have contributed," admitted Dr. Mercer, "but she wanted to move, and if it hadn't been that it could have been something else."

"Could worry cause a heart attack?"

"Was Mrs. Graham worried about anything?" asked Dr. Mercer, giving Sue a keen glance.

"She never said so, but I had a feeling that she was. I'd got to know her quite well, you see, and she was sort of different lately. Not exactly discontented, but sort of—sort of—"

Sue waved her hands about helplessly. "Oh, I don't know. It sounds so silly, but it was almost as if she had a premonition that she was going to die."

"Perhaps she had," said the doctor soothingly. "She was a very ill woman, you know. Perhaps this apprehension you are talking about was simply a realization of how very ill she was."

"I suppose that must have been it," said Sue, but she was still uneasy in her mind, and she could not help but communicate her unease to Bob, although she did not want to worry him. He was very kind about it and said many reassuring things and she felt a little better.

Nobody else seemed to share her unease. Everybody was suitably shocked, of course, and some people, including most of the residents and a few old friends of Mrs. Graham, were genuinely distressed. A cousin came down from London and disposed of her belongings, and a little group of mourners gathered in the chapel at the crematorium on a sultry, overcast afternoon.

On the evening of the day of the funeral there was an air of gloom about Digby Hall. The sky was dark with threatening thunder. Clement Horder, who was normally a contented person in spite of his disability, could not settle down to reading, but wandered out into the garden in the twilight, seeking relief among the night-scented flowers from his sense of heaviness and foreboding.

In the small sitting room on the second floor Miss Pick and Dr. Cunningham set out the chess pieces and made a few desultory moves. The windows were opened wide but it was oppressively hot and airless. Dr. Cunningham made a foolish move and then took out a handkerchief and wiped his face.

"Sorry," he said. "I'm giving you a rotten game. Must be the weather. I can't seem to concentrate."

'Neither can I." Miss Pick's responding move was

equally feeble. "Would you like anything to drink?" she asked.

"Just water, please."

This was unusual. Dr. Cunningham liked a lager, and Miss Pick normally had some cans ready in the fridge on a Friday evening. They sat sipping ice water and neither seemed to have any inclination to continue with the game.

"It'll feel strange without Mrs. Graham," said Miss Pick.

"Yes," said Dr. Cunningham briefly.

"Did you expect her to die so soon?"

"What'd you mean, so soon?"

He spoke brusquely, and Miss Pick was taken aback. Normally their chess playing was accompanied by a little gentle gossip, kept well within bounds, as indeed was the whole of their friendship.

"I don't mean anything in particular," she replied. "I suppose I was just wondering whether you'd thought she would live some months yet, or even years."

"With that condition she could have died any moment. At any moment," he repeated with emphasis.

Miss Pick, observing him carefully, was suddenly struck with an idea. She believed she could guess the reason for his unwanted moroseness.

"I do believe you're blaming yourself," she said, "because of the switching over flats. I do believe you're saying to yourself that if you hadn't changed flats with her, she might be alive now."

These remarks were rather stretching the previous limits of their friendship into something more personal, but Dr. Cunningham seemed to welcome them.

"I suppose I am, in a way," he said, "although it's quite ridiculous. I've always wanted that flat, but I'd never have dreamed of suggesting it if the first move hadn't come from her."

"In that case it's not your fault in the least."

"I know it isn't, and she could just as well have had the heart attack downstairs."

"Of course she could. And if the strain of moving was anything to do with it, that was entirely her own doing."

"All the same," said Dr. Cunningham, "I can't help wishing it hadn't happened just then."

"I wish it hadn't happened at all, but I'm trying to comfort myself by thinking that she would have hated to grow more and more weak and dependent and that it must have been a quick and easy death."

"Oh yes. It was a quick and easy death."

"Such a happy release for our poor dear Mrs. Graham, as Mrs. Langford would say so sweetly."

"Oh. Mrs. Langford." Dr. Cunningham made a face. He and Miss Pick held much the same opinion of Mrs. Langford. How had the poor husband endured that frightful simper and that sickening egoism.

"Fancy coming to the funeral in a black dress," said Miss Pick.

"I expect she thought it suited her. Do you know, I think I could fancy that lager now."

In the warden's sitting room there was an unofficial little business meeting taking place.

"We have never had this happen at Digby Hall before," said Mrs. Gurney rather as if she regarded Mrs. Graham's death as a personal insult to herself. "A death on the premises. There are some applicants on our waiting list who would not want to move into that apartment. People can be very superstitious, you know."

She paused and looked at the three other people in the room as if daring them to contradict her. Sue and Bob Merry, who were feeling tired and depressed, had no inclination to argue or to do anything that could prolong the discussion. Mr. Ernest Fisher, a spare, dark, tight-looking man, said nothing because he was reserving his forces for the battle that he knew was coming.

"It's very difficult to stop people talking," continued Mrs. Gurney, looking severely at her three silent listeners. "We don't want any new residents to hear anything that might distress them. No suggestion that there was any neglect, for example."

Sue Merry, who was sitting beside her husband on the

settee, gripped its edge with a convulsive movement of the hand. Bob put his hand gently over hers. Neither of them spoke.

"I am not suggesting for a moment that there was any such thing," went on Mrs. Gurney. "Mrs. Graham was a very sick woman, and in my opinion she ought to have been removed to hospital before her condition had deteriorated so far." She glared at Mr. Fisher, who remained impassive. "However, there is nothing to be done about that now. All we can do is ensure that we do not make any further mistakes."

"There's no way we can stop people becoming ill and dying," said Bob so mildly and politely that even Mrs. Gurney could scarcely suspect him of insolence. Sue's hand was trembling again and he hoped she would feel a little better if he put in this remark. He didn't like Sue being in this nervous state, and he longed for the whole business to be over and done with so that they could get back to normal.

"We are not expecting you to alter the course of nature, Mr. Merry," said Mrs. Gurney with heavy irony. "I am simply pointing out the sort of considerations that should be taken into account when offering the vacant apartment to one of the applicants on the waiting list."

This was the moment for Mr. Fisher to come into action. "At the inaugural meeting of this Association," he said, "it was decided that a list should be kept of those applicants approved by the Committee for an apartment in one of our residences, and that vacancies should be offered to applicants strictly in accordance with their position on that list. Exceptions were to be made only when an applicant's personal circumstances were such as to warrant a jumping of the queue."

Mrs. Gurney began to speak, but Mr. Fisher rolled on relentlessly. He had a surprisingly strong voice for such a small man and had behind him many years of commanding the attention of underlings.

"In my opinion, this rule has already been broken far too often on the most flimsy of pretexts."

"If you are thinking of Mrs. Langford," said Mrs. Gurney equally firmly, "may I remind you that I was away at the time it was decided to offer her the place at Digby Hall. Had I been present at that Committee meeting I should certainly have opposed the suggestion."

"And so should I, Mrs. Gurney," said Mr. Fisher, "but, unfortunately, I could not attend that meeting either."

"It was most improper. There was no reason whatever why Mrs. Langford should have taken precedence over all the other applicants."

"No reason at all, except that her son happened to be very friendly with our president," said Mr. Fisher drily.

"A perfectly healthy woman, in comfortable circumstances, and with a good home."

"Exactly. But here she is and we cannot turn her out. At any rate, there is one thing to be said for Mrs. Langford. She is hardly likely to cause us the embarrassment of dying on the premises in the near future."

The temporary truce was at an end and Mr. Fisher was not going to give Mrs. Gurney any help at all in bringing out her suggestion. She was obliged to plunge straight in.

"The next name on the list is Mrs. Price, who applied only very shortly before Miss Dawson, who follows her. Mrs. Price is a delightful lady, but she has a rather nervous disposition, whereas Miss Dawson is thoroughly sensible and well balanced. I happen to know her personally."

"Yes, Mrs. Gurney, I think we all know that you happen to know Miss Dawson personally."

One up to Mr. Fisher, thought Bob Merry; he's going to win this round. Normally, he and Sue listened to these discussions with amusement, laying bets on who would win. Today, however, Bob was only mildly interested in the outcome, and Sue did not care what happened at all. She had a bad headache and the room seemed to be getting more and more airless. If only this thunderstorm would break at last. If only these people would go.

They went at last. Bob accompanied them to their cars, parked in the drive outside the main entrance. There was still no sign of rain. When he came back to the warden's flat he said: "It's going to be Mrs. Price, I think. The Gurney is not up to her usual form. I suppose trying to wangle her old schoolfriend in is rather—"

He broke off. Sue was curled up in a corner of the settee, pressing her fingers to her temples and quivering. Bob stiffened, made a slight gesture of impatience, and then controlled himself enough to try to soothe her. After a while his efforts seemed to have some effect.

"If only Mrs. Graham had told me what was worrying her," said Sue, "then I shouldn't feel so bad. I might have been able to help. But to think that she died full of some awful worry—"

The tears threatened again.

"It's all over, love," said Bob. "She died peacefully. She didn't suffer. Everyone agrees on that."

"But she'd suffered before. It's as if something was threatening her. Oh Bob, I do wish we could move from here straightaway!"

"But darling, we have to give three months' notice. And where else are we going to get a flat?"

"I know. I'm sorry. Of course we can't leave Digby Hall yet."

"Shall we see if anybody else knows what was worrying Mrs. Graham. How about Dr. Cunningham?"

Sue shook her head. "He's feeling guilty about changing flats himself?"

"Mrs. Langford?"

Sue made a face. "Definitely no. I'm certainly not going to discuss Mrs. Graham with Mrs. Langford." She got up. "The only thing is to try and forget it. Mrs. Gurney's right about that, if nothing else. The less said about it the better."

"Just another tenny bit, please, Lorna." Amy gave her little giggle. "That's enough." She put a hand over her glass. "I'm getting quite tiddly."

But it was Mrs. Ramsden, not Mrs. Langford, who was getting tiddly. Oppressed by the funeral and by the weather, she had taken refuge in her favourite gin, and had drunk at least four times as much as Amy.

"I ought not to have this really," she said at frequent intervals. "The doctor warned me. It doesn't mix with my tablets."

"Why shouldn't you drink when you're taking medicines?" said Amy with an air of innocent enquiry. "I've often wondered."

"Because the alcohol enhances the effect of the drug. You have to watch it with patients who are confused or depressed. We had quite a lot of those in the nursing home."

"But how did they get hold of the alcohol? Surely you didn't give it to them?"

"Got their visitors to smuggle it in. You'd never believe, my dear, the tricks they get up to."

"Oh really? Do tell me more about your nursing home. I'm sure you and your husband must have got very fed up with some of the patients sometimes. Did you ever feel like giving them an overdose to keep them quiet?"

This was very daring, but it was said in a jokey tone of voice and was followed by a most attentive and flattering silence. Mrs. Ramsden became voluble. Mrs. Langford listened for some time.

Eventually Mrs. Ramsden gave a great yawn. "Must be the weather," she said. "I do wish this storm would break."

It's not the weather, said Amy to herself; it's because you're more than half drunk, you silly old bitch. Aloud she said that it probably was the sultry air that was making dear Lorna feel so sleepy. "I'll leave you in peace," she added, getting up. "It's been a tiring day."

Mrs. Ramsden agreed. "Wonder who they'll put in the empty flat," she said as Amy prepared to depart.

"I believe Mr. Merry mentioned a Mrs. Price," said Amy.

She did not add that this information had been obtained by eavesdropping. Bob and Sue had been clearing up in Mrs. Graham's apartment late the previous evening. The curtains had been drawn across the window that opened onto the balcony, but it was surprising how much you could hear of what went on inside when you put your ear to the glass. Amy was getting very adept at climbing over the low rail that separated her section of the balcony from that belonging to the neighbouring flat. Of course one had to wait until after dark, and even then there was some risk that she might be noticed from below. The headlamps of a car coming up the drive, for example, might throw enough light on that side of the house for her to be seen.

"Mrs. Price," muttered Lorna Ramsden. "Another dreary old woman, I suppose. Pity we can't have someone interesting."

'Well, dear, there are always more women than men. And after all, you have got me!'

Mrs. Ramsden became somewhat maudlin. Of course she meant no reflection on her dear friend Amy. It had made all the difference in the world of life at Digby Hall to have Amy Langford there.

"Thank you," said Amy. "I do rather flatter myself that I have livened things up a bit."

Lorna Ramsden agreed. "Come again soon," she added.

"Thank you, dear, but it's my turn to do the entertaining. You know what we agreed."

They fixed an evening. As soon as she was back in her own quarters Amy followed the set expression on her face to fall apart. These tête-à-têtes with Lorna Ramsden were becoming a bore. The woman was stupid and crude. Her malice was only superficial and easily gratified. She had none of the courage of real hatred in her, and could become revoltingly sentimental on the slightest provocation. On the other hand, she was very useful as a source of information, and there might be occasions when she could be an essential, if unwitting, accomplice.

Amy could not decide whether to exempt Lorna from the fate that was being planned for everybody else at Digby Hall. Perhaps it would be best to leave the matter open for the time being. After all, she would eventually have to decide about Mrs. Price, and all the others who would be brought in at some later date to fill the vacancies as they arose. On the other hand, Lorna herself had described such a very simple and undetectable way for Amy to do away with her that it seemed a pity to waste it.

Perhaps it could be used on one of the others. It would have to be someone who took in a lot of alcohol. George Cunningham? But he never got drunk, and he was a doctor and by no means stupid or careless. There were big problems there. Did he take any pills or tablets regularly? It might be worth finding out.

Amy was very thoughtful as she appeared to go to bed. She was standing naked, just about to put on her night-dress, when the storm broke at last with an enormous clap of thunder. The relief of tension let loose some elemental force in her. Scarcely knowing what she was doing, she switched off the light, pulled back the curtains, flung wide the casements, and held her hands out into the torrential rain. The force of it filled her with excitement. She was as powerful as the rain, as terrifying as the thunder, as dangerous as the lightning. Everyone was at her mercy. She was wonderful. Sublime. Divine.

She put her hands onto the windowsill and in the next lightning flash saw them for a split second white sparkling. Then she raised them to her shoulders and hugged herself in an ecstasy of adoration. It was a long time before the mood died away and she was able to put on her nightgown and renew her promise to the sweet image in the mirror.

"But you must try to be patient, my precious," she whispered. "I shall have to wait a little now, just to be on the safe side. Besides, I am not sure yet which is to be the next. It will depend how things go. I have so many schemes—I will tell you all about them, but you must let me take my time. I can't do everything at once."

She continued to whisper to the image for several minutes, apologising to it, almost pleading with it. It seemed as if the image was displeased. It did not smile in quite the charming and appealing way that it had smiled before. The mouth seemed to have lost its softness, the eyes their gentleness.

"Don't be angry with me, Amy," she murmured to the mirror. "I will be good in future, I promise. I ought not to have behaved like that in the thunderstorm. Something just seemed to come over me. I must have been mad. I'll try not to get like that again.''

When at last the features seemed to have relaxed she leant forward for the good-night kiss. Then she crept into bed, suddenly so exhausted that she could barely move, switched out the light, and lay there motionless, as if in a coma, but not asleep. Everything seemed to be jumbled up in a kaleidoscopic series of images and impressions: Mrs. Graham's white dead face and Lorna Ramsden's coarse dark living one; the lightning and the rain and the lashing trees; the sweet mirror Amy and the tremendous goddess of power with the wet sparkling hands.

All of them came round and round relentlessly; shattering, mixing together, then separating again.

But Mrs. Langford was by no means the only person at Digby Hall to remain wakeful that night.

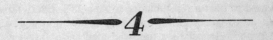

4

Mr. Clement Horder had always been a very placid man. He was respected by his colleagues, well-liked by his acquaintances, and had never hated anybody. There were, however, two big loves in his life. One was botany and the other was his wife. After her death his deafness became much worse and he told his son and daughter-in-law that he would rather live in some quiet residential home than join their busy, restless household in North London. Digby Hall suited him perfectly, the family were satisfied, and they all met together once a month and at Christmas.

Clement Horder neither looked forward to these meetings nor dreaded them. Since Angela's death all people were alike to him, even his own folks, his own grandchildren. Of course they did not know this. Nobody knew how little they mattered, how little he differentiated between one human face and another. He was naturally courteous and his deafness protected him from close human contact and from giving offence by his indifference.

When somebody attempted to break through the barrier, as Mrs. Ramsden had done with her efforts to change library books and shop and cook for him, he responded up to a

point, but sooner or later they would be obliged to give up
the struggle. Mrs. Graham's death had distressed him
because that was how Angela had died. In her sleep, of
heart failure. Everyone had said it was a mercy, such a
peaceful way to go, but Clement could not feel that at all.
All he knew was that he was going to spend the rest of his
life searching for her.

Shut up in his own silent world, insulated from the tumult
of life, he could use his eyes, which functioned very well,
in trying to find her likeness. The only time when one
human face stood out from all the others was when it
seemed to bear a resemblance to Angela's. Every now and
then he caught a glimpse of such a face and it gave him
fresh hope. In between times he read and thought and ate
and slept and smiled at anyone who spoke to him, and went
for long walks over the downs looking for wild flowers.

He was neither happy nor unhappy. He was simply
waiting. Time had stood still since Angela's death, but it
could not stand still forever. It would come to an end one
day.

When Amy Langford came to live at Digby Hall,
Clement Horder had the feeling that time had begun to
move again. His search was over. Or rather, as nearly over
as it was ever likely to be. For his mind was not in the least
bit disordered or unbalanced by his great loss. Clement
Horder knew perfectly well that Angela was dead and that
he would never see her again in this life. He knew that his
search was only for a woman whose face resembled hers,
nothing more. What he did not know was what would
become of him, how he would react, if this craving was
ever satisfied.

The nose is wrong, he said to himself while studying
Amy across the dining table, but it doesn't show except in
profile. The eyes are like; the mouth is very like. The hair
ought to be longer, and a little more untidy sometimes. And
a more natural grey. I wonder if I might suggest it? The blue
dress will do, but the necklace must go. Shall I suggest that
too?

Clement Horder had smiled at his own thoughts. Of

course he knew that he was not looking at Angela, but at some strange woman who had taken up residence at Digby Hall. What on earth would she think if he went to ask her to discard her jewellery and refrain from tinting and setting her hair in order that she might more closely resemble his dead wife!

He laughed at himself. He had to share his little jokes with himself because his deafness made it so difficult for him to share them with others.

In spite of her deficiencies, Mr. Horder enjoyed looking at the newcomer to Digby Hall. He was careful not to stare too much because he did not want to draw attention to himself and he had no more desire to get to know the strange lady then he had to get to know anybody else. But as the days passed by, the sight of her became more and more important to him. He actually noticed if she was not present at the midday meal, or if she spent less time than usual sitting on the sun terrace. Clement Horder was far from being unobservant. If for the most part he did not see what went on at Digby Hall, it was purely because he was not interested.

After Mrs. Langford's arrival his attitude changed. It is impossible to seek for a certain plant without paying some attention to all those other plants for which one is not seeking. The same with a human face. In looking around for the face that was like Angela's, Clement Horder inevitably noticed rather more of all those faces that were not like Angela's.

This was how he came to be aware that the frail little old lady was seen less and less outside her own apartment, and how he came to learn from Bob Merry, with whom he could most easily communicate, about Mrs. Graham's illness and the manner of her death.

On the evening of the day of the funeral he spent a long time in the garden trying to calm himself and trying to decide whether or not to speak to the lady with Angela's face and warn her that those little balconies outside the first-floor windows of the house were for decoration, at the most to support a few flowerpots, and not for people to stand on.

Three times in the late evening he had seen her standing right out on the flimsy little structure, actually leaning on the rail or moving about on the balcony.

It had been too dark to see her face, but she had Angela's figure too: a little taller and plumper; that was all. The first time he had seen her there Clement Horder had had quite a shock. It had upset his mental balance, and for one crazy moment he had the notion that Angela herself had come out there to look for him, to call him in from the garden as she had so often done in their life together.

The fancy had soon vanished, and after that all his concern had been for the lady herself. That balcony was not made to bear her weight. She really must not take such risks. There could be a very nasty accident indeed, and among all the other unplesant results he, Clement Horder, would lose the pleasure of seeing Angela's face.

On the evening after Mrs. Graham's funeral he did not see Mrs. Langford come out on the balcony. He came indoors before the first thunderclap and went to bed but not to sleep. By morning he had decided that he would have to speak to her himself and not do it through Bob Merry. After all, the lady did have a life and character of her own, and she deserved to be treated as an individual in her own right and not just as his vision of Angela.

He would have to get out the hearing aid that he hated to use because no aid was well suited to his condition and it broke into his peace; but he could not endure to have people bawling uselessly at him, and he could hardly expect her to write down what she wanted to say, as young Bob Merry always did.

For the next few days Mr. Horder sought in vain for an opportunity to speak to Mrs. Langford. She always disappeared immediately after the midday meal, and was little seen in the garden, the weather having been damp and cool since the big storm. Neither did Mr. Horder see her on the balcony again when he strolled round the house in the late evening, but that didn't necessarily mean she had stopped taking this silly risk, and he was still determined to speak to her.

In fact, Amy was deliberately lying low, trying to regain her balance after that extraordinary experience on the night of the big thunderstorm, and also trying to decide about Lorna Ramsden, who was becoming more and more of a nuisance. The balcony was not at the moment of any interest to her, since nobody had yet moved into the neighbouring flat. Mrs. Gurney was apparently still trying to secure it for her friend, and Amy played her part in the gossip, but without taking sides, as some of the others were inclined to do. Whether her new neighbour was to be Mrs. Price or Miss Dawson was not of great importance. Whichever it was, Amy would soon discover the weak spots, since every human being had weak spots, and file them away to make use of when the occasion arose.

Mrs. Ramsden, however, was intensely interested in the matter, perhaps fearing that another arrival could intrude upon her friendship with Amy Langford, and it was to get away from Lorna one day that Amy walked up the sloping lawn to the shrubbery and sat on the seat beside the lilac bushes. Mr. Horder, who was halfway up the drive and about to take advantage of the fine morning to go for one of his downland walks, changed his mind when he saw his chance.

"Nice morning, Mrs. Langford," he said, beaming upon her.

She looked up, smiled and nodded, but did not attempt to reply. Mr. Horder was of no concern to her at this moment. Her mind was full of the plan to eliminate Lorna Ramsden. It was foolproof and complete, but it had better wait for another couple of weeks because it would be inadvisable to have two deaths at Digby Hall within a month. Meanwhile she could be thinking about Miss Pick, who was a daily irritant with her red nose and her straggly hair and her brusqueness and horribly energetic cheerfulness.

No doubt Miss Pick had her weakness, but up till now Amy had not succeeded in uncovering them. Mending fences, digging in the kitchen garden, even poking about under Dr. Cunningham's car—Miss Pick was always doing something, and it seemed that she did it properly and was not simply interfering or trying to attract attention. Would it be possible for her to have an accident? A fall from a stepladder, for instance, when she was doing some decorating. Or perhaps she would be taking part in the cutting back of some of the trees in the drive. There were possibilities there.

"May I share your seat?"

The voice startled Amy. She had been concentrating on the challenge of Miss Pick and had completely forgotten Mr. Horder. It was most unusual for him to linger. Normally he would make his little comment and walk on in his steady, dignified manner. There were times when she almost envied him his deafness. It excused him from having to listen to Lorna Ramsden, for one thing.

But it also made him very exhausting company on the few occasions when it was necessary to convey a message to him. Amy smiled an invitation to him to sit down, but her heart sank at the thought of trying to converse. On the other hand, it would look too rude to get up and go away immediately. Amy still behaved politely to everybody she came in contact with, but it was a matter of policy, not of faith, for she now believed in nothing except the wonderful, limitless power of Amy.

"A fine specimen of daphne," said Mr. Horder. "I am surprised that it grows so well on this chalky soil."

Amy withdrew her eyes from the bush at which she had been staring and once more smiled and nodded.

"You are a keen gardener?" persisted Mr. Horder.

There is a limit to the amount of silent smiling and nodding that one can do. When asked a question, the natural impulse is to reply to it in speech. Even wonderful Amy was no exception to this rule.

"I'm not much of a gardener," she said in her normal voice, not particularly loudly, "but I am very fond of flowers."

To her great surprise Mr. Horder appeared to understand her, and a conversation followed concerning gardens, Mr. Horder's dislike of using a hearing aid, and Mrs. Ramsden.

Amy hastily adjusted herself to this unexpected human contact and turned her mind to the new possibilities that it opened up. There might well be some way in which she could make use of Mr. Horder before his own turn came to be eliminated. At the very least, it would be worth cultivating him in order to make Lorna jealous.

"I hope I am not keeping you from joining your friend," said Mr. Horder.

"My friend?" Amy was at a loss.

"I think I have sometimes seen you go out with Mrs. Ramsden." As he said this Mr. Horder hoped that it did not sound too interfering. He was using the remark as a sort of dress rehearsal, so to speak, for the much more interfering comments that were his object in this encounter. To his relief, the woman with Angela's face did not take offence, but actually laughed lightly.

"I wouldn't exactly call Mrs. Ramsden a friend. I felt rather lonely when I came here and she has been kind to me. But a friend—I don't know that I've got any friends."

Amy regretted these last words the moment she had spoken. It was not the sort of thing the old Amy, Philip's Amy, sweet image in the mirror Amy, would have said. The remark belonged to the ecstatic Amy of the thunderstorm, the Amy who must at all costs be kept hidden from all other human beings. Fortunately, no harm was done on this occasion. Indeed, the remark seemed to go down well with Mr. Horder.

"I think we all use the term far too loosely," he was saying. "I think it is very honest of you—unusually honest, if I may say so—not to describe Mrs. Ramsden as a friend."

How very strange, Clement Horder was saying to himself, that this woman with Angela's face should have Angela's directness too. A sensible woman. Much more so than he would have thought from the little he had noticed of her, apart from her face, up till this morning.

Amy said nothing. The old self and the new self were warring uncomfortably within her, and somewhere in the midst of the battle there seemed to be yet another Amy, quite different from either the old or the new, a little frail young green shoot of an Amy that pushed up hopefully between the rival powers and that was warmed and refreshed by Mr. Horder's compliment.

Unusually honest. It was like sunshine and showers to this tiny sprouting seed of an Amy. It caused her to glance at him in such a way that for one fatal fleeting moment Clement Horder saw Angela's character look out of the eyes that were so like Angela's, and he heard himself speak in a tone of voice that he had never expected to use to any human being again.

"I hope you will come to feel that you can look on me as a friend, Mrs. Langford."

They were the wrong words for the little frail plant. Perhaps at this moment no words would have been the right ones. The old Amy who had believed that all homage was her due and the new Amy who despised and used all creatures in her powerful urge to destroy, came together in an unholy alliance to crush the little seed of truth.

"I hope I will, Mr. Horder," she said, modestly averting her eyes while excited thoughts of new realms of power began to stir in her mind. I'll get him to take me for a drive, she said to herself. I know he hires a car now and then. And I'll make sure that Lorna sees us go. But there was no need to angle for the invitation, because he was actually suggesting it himself.

Apparently they had been talking about wild flowers again while her thoughts had been racing ahead, and she must have been making encouraging remarks, expressing a desire to see this rare type of orchid that grew in the meadows along the riverbank in a remote part of the county. A day and time were suggested. What better than tomorrow, provided the weather held? Was Mrs. Langford free?

The old Amy wanted to make some coy pretence of not being available at such short notice. The all-powerful Amy wanted to test her ascendancy by making him choose another day. But this time in their struggle they destroyed each other and left the way open for the truth to spring up again.

"I'm always free," said Amy, "and I'd love to come tomorrow."

Clement Horder expressed his delight.

"Will you think me very rude," he added, touching the hearing aid, "if I switch this thing off now?"

"Of course not," said Amy. "As a matter of fact, there's some shopping I have to do, so if you'll excuse me—"

They reverted to smiles and nods for the parting.

Clement Horder withdrew into his silent world but found no peace there. The incredible had happened. He had made contact with another human being again and there was to be further contact. He ought to have been full of excited anticipation. Certainly he was extremely agitated, but there was more of pain than of pleasure in it. What on earth had led him to do such a crazy thing? He who had so withdrawn from human society that he scarcely knew any longer how to converse, had let himself in for spending several hours alone with a woman of whom he knew nothing.

How could he get through those hours? He began to worry about them, minute by minute. The driving would not be too bad, because he would explain to her that with his disability it took every bit of his concentration and it would be positively dangerous to try to talk. The actual looking for specimens of marsh orchid would also be comparatively simple, except that the place he was thinking of could be rather damp and it might well be that she would not really be happy to scramble about on a muddy riverbank, but would agree to it just to please him. He would have to study her carefully and try to find out what she really wanted.

What could he do if it seemed to him that she did not feel like joining him on the little walk from the parking place to the edge of the river? It was an unfrequented spot, well off the main tourist routes, and had no amenities, not even a bench to sit on. He would have to leave her sitting in the car while he searched for the orchids, which would look rather discourteous, but there would be no help for it.

And then there was the question of tea. For himself he would usually put in a thermos flask and a sandwich for such excursions, but Mrs. Langford would surely expect to

be taken out to tea, and he would want to treat her
handsomely. The trouble was that there was no suitable
place, in fact no place at all, in that isolated neighbourhood.
They might even have to drive back to the coast again, and
there would be parking difficulties, and the tea shops and
hotels would be crowded with holidaymakers.

It was in vain that Clement Horder told himself he was
being absurd in thus fretting like a teenager over a date with
the first girl who had ever looked at him. Knowing how
ridiculous it was for a man of his age to go on like this did
not stop him doing it. He continued to worry over the
forthcoming excursion, minute by minute, and it was at
least an hour after the talk with Mrs. Langford before he
remembered that he had not mentioned the danger of her
using the balcony.

Amy Langford also became very agitated as a result of
the conversation in the shrubbery. Had it taken place
immediately after her arrival at Digby Hall she would have
reacted quite differently. Mr. Horder, even though deaf,
would have been welcomed as an admirer. But she had
changed so much since then. It was with incredulity, as well
as with surprise, that she recalled the little daydream that
she had spun about Mr. Horder. The woman who had built
up that daydream seemed to belong to another life and it
was becoming harder and harder for Amy Langford, all-
powerful avenger and destroyer, to camouflage herself
under that earlier Amy's skin.

On the other hand, she had been gratified, genuinely
gratified and not just pleased to get Mr. Horder into her
power, when he had praised her honesty. This was what
made it all so confusing. It was certainly not the thunderstorm Amy whom he was praising, because nobody else
except herself knew of that woman's existence. Nobody else
now alive, perhaps she ought to say. Mrs. Graham had seen
that other Amy in those few seconds when her eyes had
stared through the transparent polythene at her nighttime
visitor, and her crippled hands, tucked tightly under the
bedclothes, could make no attempt to protect herself. But
the mortal remains of Mrs. Graham had been consumed by

the furnace at the crematorium, and the record stated that she had died of heart failure. Nobody would ever have the faintest suspicion.

Nobody would ever have the faintest suspicion that Mrs. Ramsden's death, when it took place, was anything but an accident brought about by her own carelessness in consuming large quantities of alcohol in addition to her strong tranquillisers. People were dying every day from an injudicious mixture of drink and drugs. Lorna Ramsden was just the type of person to be such a victim.

And if Lorna had had a disappointment—if, for example, she had seen Amy Langford carry off Mr. Horder under her very nose—then she would be all the more likely to seek solace in gin. How beautifully it all fitted together! Amy the omnipotent schemer was delighted. The trouble was that the other Amys kept popping up and disturbing her satisfaction.

Sometimes she sank back into the woman she had once been, who had spun a daydream about the distinguished-looking elderly gentleman who was to be her protector and worshipper. The trouble was that it did not seem as attractive as it had before. Where was the fun in being taken care of and adored, compared with the feeling of holding the destiny of other people in your hands?

At other times she could hear Mr. Horder's voice quite clearly in her mind. Unusually honest. The words brought an odd little thrill, as if a curtain had suddenly been drawn aside to reveal a new world. It was enticing but it was also dangerous. One glimpse of it was enough to make the other two Amys band together.

"Oh Amy, my precious, I am so terribly muddled!" said Amy when she talked to her mirror image that evening. "It was all going so well and now I seem to have lost my way. What shall I do?"

The face stared back at her, pretty and charming still, but with a puzzled and anxious expression.

"Oh, don't look like that! I can't bear to see you so unhappy," she cried, putting up her hands to cover her eyes.

"I ought not to be bringing you my problems," she went

on presently. "I'm better now. Don't worry, my sweet. You shall have your revenge."

She dropped her hands. Amy in the mirror looked more as she ought to look, but still not completely at peace.

"I told you I might have to change the plan from time to time," pleaded Amy's voice.

The image began to soften, to take on a forgiving look, and Amy began to feel a little better.

It did not last for long. Right in the middle of one of her soothing reassurances Amy saw the image suddenly take on the worried expression again, and this time it was worse than ever. The mouth was dragged down in a very ugly way; the eyes were wide open, frightened and wild.

Once again Amy raised her hands, this time not to cover her eyes but to place them, palms downwards, against the glass to blot out the image.

"I can't help you," she cried aloud. "I don't know what to do. I know you want me to kill Mr. Horder, because he disappointed you so badly. But I don't want to kill him. I want to be his friend. I like him. And he likes me!"

She made one hand into a fist and banged it on the glass.

"I won't kill him!" Her voice was rising. She was almost shouting now and could not stop herself. "I like him and he likes me!"

She turned her back on the mirror and bit at her finger to try to stop her crying. It was at that moment, in the sudden silence, that she thought she heard the sound of movement in the house. She rushed across the big room and opened the door of the apartment. There was nobody on the landing nor on the stairs, nobody just disappearing through another door, nobody in the foyer-lounge below. Perhaps she had imagined it. Or perhaps it had come from the neighbouring flat. Mrs. Graham had never made a sound, but when Dr. Cunningham had been her neighbour Amy had sometimes heard him moving about.

Supposing there was someone there now? Bob or Sue Merry, or even the new resident? Suppose they had heard her talking to herself? Suppose they had actually heard what she said?

You must snap out of this, said some part of Amy, coming to the rescue of the trembling creature standing panic-stricken in the middle of the room. Turn the radio up loud. Or the television. People will think that is what they heard.

She moved over to the television, and the sudden noise of gunfire and screaming made her jump. Hastily she adjusted the sound. Mustn't draw attention to herself by breaking the rules of Digby Hall. For ten minutes Amy sat in front of the screen, half-expecting somebody to come and complain.

Nothing happened. No knock, no call on the internal phone. It was as if she was the only human being in the place. She got up and switched off the television, suddenly feeling very lonely and longing to hear the sound of human activity nearby. How could she find out whether there really was somebody in the flat next door? Either by going out onto the landing and knocking or by telephoning the warden's flat. Both of these methods would draw attention to herself.

Amy was fairly calm now, but there might still be something in her appearance that would give her away. It would be a good idea to go and check in the mirror, but she was frightened of the mirror image after the way it had been playing tricks with her this evening. Was there no other means of finding out whether someone had moved in next door?

Of course there was. The balcony. It was getting late, and to eyes adjusted to a well-lit room there seemed to be very little light left in the sky. Of course the long window next door would be bolted, but she didn't want to go in, only to see if there was a light, or whether she could hear any sound. In fact, she didn't even need to climb over the partition: stepping just outside her own long window would be enough.

The curtains were still drawn back and there was no light and nothing to be heard. The apartment was emtpy. It was more than likely that it had been empty all evening and Amy had only imagined the sound of movement.

Unless it was a ghost.

Nonsense. She didn't believe in ghosts. Mrs. Graham was gone forever.

Amy shut all her windows and drew the curtains across and settled down in front of the television, forcing herself to attend to the programme. The panic was rising again, and if she didn't take a firm grip on herself she was going to get no sleep and she would be quite unfit for the next day's excursion with her friend Mr. Horder.

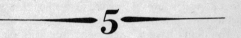

5

At half-past ten the following morning Mrs. Ramsden, having waited in vain for Mrs. Langford to join her in the foyer, came upstairs again and knocked on the latter's door. There was no reply. She knocked again and waited, half-impatient, half-anxious. You never knew. There might be something wrong. Amy was very tough, for all she liked to put on that helpless air. But all the same, you never knew. People could have heart attacks even if they weren't heart patients like Mrs. Graham. Or people could drink too much. Or swallow too many sleeping pills.

You never knew. Lorna Ramsden thoroughly enjoyed Amy's company. She had certainly livened up this old morgue a bit. It would be a pity if anything had happened to her, but it would also be rather exciting, and any sort of excitement was better than none.

"Hullo, Mrs. Ramsden," said Sue Merry, coming along the landing from the warden's quarters. "If you're waiting for Mrs. Langford, I'm afraid she's gone out. I've just seen her going down the drive."

"Then I've missed her. What a shame. I thought she might like to come shopping."

"Perhaps she won't be long." Sue gave Mrs. Ramsden a quick smile and hurried on downstairs.

Mrs. Ramsden was disappointed. She had hoped for a little chat. The girl looks worried, she said to herself; she's not been the same since Mrs. Graham died. A natural death if ever there was one, but all the same . . . Could there possibly be anything else behind it? Did Mrs. Merry know something that she was not telling? It was, after all, Sue who had found Mrs. Graham dead. Had she removed some telltale evidence? A half-empty bottle of tablets, for example?

Lorna Ramsden looked forward to another chat with Amy about this new idea of hers. That was the nice thing about Amy. You didn't have to watch what you said. Not like all these other stuffy people at Digby Hall. On the other hand, there were things about Amy that Lorna did not quite like. This going off without letting her know, for instance. It was true that they had not fixed to go shopping together this morning, but Lorna had said she was going, and Amy had not said that she wouldn't join her. So naturally she had assumed . . . There was something rather secretive about Amy sometimes. And a rather funny look in her eye. It reminded Lorna of that senile old woman they had once had in the nursing home who had gone completely off her head and run about the house stark naked, smashing cups and saucers and anything else she could lay her hands on.

Now that really would be exciting, thought Lorna Ramsden as she set out alone on her shopping expedition, if Amy Langford were to go completely off her head.

Sue Merry hovered behind the half-open dining-room door until she was sure that Mrs. Ramsden had left the house and then came out into the foyer again, hoping to catch Mr. Horder, who usually emerged from his apartment at about this time. She had taken a telephone message from his son, and wanted to deliver it in person. It was not very important and there was no reason why she should not simply leave a note under his door, but ever since Mrs. Graham's death Sue had become almost obsessionally anxious about such little matters. She knew it was absurd, and Bob was getting more and more impatient with her, but she couldn't help it.

She puffed up the cushions in the armchairs, brushed the fallen rose petals from around the bowl on the wide windowsill, and then Mr. Horder appeared at the door of his flat. Sue ran across and touched his arm, took out the message from the pocket of her jeans, and handed it to him. He read it, smiled and nodded, and was about to walk on when he suddenly seemed to recollect something.

"Oh. Mrs. Merry. I've a message for you too."

"A message for me?" echoed Sue, knowing he could not hear, but unable to stop herself from speaking.

"It's from Mrs. Langford." He took out a piece of paper from his jacket pocket, glanced at it, and then put it back without offering to show it to Sue. "She asks me to tell you that she won't be in to lunch today. She's gone into town to do some errands and will have a snack somewhere."

"Oh. Thank you," said Sue. "I wonder why she didn't tell me herself." The fact disturbed her, as did anything the least bit out of the ordinary. Everything seemed loaded with apprehension.

Mr. Horder replied as if he had heard what she said. "That is only part of what she writes. The rest concerns an arrangement of ours." He hesitated a moment. It was no business of the young warden what the residents did with their time, provided they gave notice if they were going to be out for the midday meal or away for the night, but Mr. Horder's anxiety about the afternoon's excursion had reached such a pitch that he had to mention it to somebody.

"I am hiring a car to take Mrs. Langford botanising this afternoon," he said. "She writes that she will bring a picnic bag, but I still feel that I should take her out to tea. What do you think, Mrs. Merry? Just a minute—I will switch on my hearing aid. There. I can hear you now."

During the few seconds of waiting, all Sue's separate strands of unease had come together into a great knot of apprehension. She felt almost as protective towards Mr. Horder as she had felt towards Mrs. Graham, and the thought that Mrs. Langford had got her claws into him was intolerable. Presumably she had been doing her poor little helpless woman act with the poor old man, who only wanted to be left in peace, and had pushed him into this, pretending to be interested in wild flowers. As if a woman like Mrs. Langford would ever be interested in anything except herself!

She must have been working very secretly, though, because neither Sue nor Bob had noticed it. They had seen Mrs. Langford become friendly with Mrs. Ramsden after Mrs. Graham died, but that did not worry Sue, who did not much like Mrs. Ramsden either. In fact, if any of the women residents were pestering Mr. Horder, Sue would have thought Mrs. Ramsden was that one.

Mr. Horder was waiting for her to reply. He had made a special effort to her. She heard her own voice, falsely bright.

"You've got a lovely day for it. I hope you enjoy yourselves. I shouldn't worry about the tea, Mr. Horder. I expect Mrs. Langford realised that you might be going rather off the beaten track, and that's why she's bringing a picnic."

Mr. Horder looked a little more cheerful.

"She probably thinks of it as her contribution, as a way of saying thank you," went on Sue, and added some more complimentary remarks about Mrs. Langford, assuaging her own guilt for her dislike for that lady and perhaps trying to convince herself that it would be good for Mr. Horder to have a woman friend.

Mr. Horder certainly looked very convinced, either because he just wanted to be, or because a hearing aid is not very good at picking up subtleties and insincerities of speech.

"Well, I'll be off to see about the car," he said, and walked away with a brisk and cheerful step.

Sue stared after him, feeling on the verge of tears. Perhaps this really was the start of a romance. It would not be the first time that a late marriage had come out of a meeting in an old people's home. In fact she and Bob had sometimes wondered whether such a thing would ever happen at Digby Hall. Mr. Horder was obviously very happy; presumably Mrs. Langford was also very happy, and if her interest in his own interests was largely put on, surely she would have the sense to keep up the pretence enough to make him believe it. There would be no advantage to herself in not doing so.

All the time she was preparing the midday meal, Sue tried to stifle her sense of foreboding. Only five of them in all instead of eight. That was nothing very unusual, particularly during the summer months, when residents were often out for the day or away on visits. Nevertheless, it seemed to her an ill omen as she set out the five little glass dishes for the dessert. It was to be a lemon soufflé, a particular favourite. For Sue Merry the elderly residents were like a family. Naturally, she liked some of them more than the others, but nevertheless it was terrible to have them dropping off like this, one by one.

But they aren't dropping off one by one, you fool, she told herself angrily. Mrs. Graham has died, which everybody expected to happen soon, and Mrs. Langford is having a snack lunch in town, which she has every right to have, and she has probably arranged to meet Mr. Horder at the garage, or somewhere else away from Digby Hall, so that they can go off without anybody seeing them, and I don't blame them for that at all. If I were them, I'd do just the same.

Thus Sue Merry comforted herself. In fact, she was quite right about the meeting place. At two-thirty Mr. Horder collected his usual Ford Cortina from the garage that was about ten minutes walk away from Digby Hall, and found Mrs. Langford already there, sitting on the only chair in the little office and looking very cool and summery in her blue dress. On the floor beside her was a shopping basket out of which protruded the top of a thermos flask.

"I won't tell you what else I've got," she said as she greeted him. "I've been going mad at Fletchers."

Fletchers was the best baker in town. Mr. Horder, who was using his hearing aid while he transacted his business at the garage, caught the name but not the rest of her remark. I

do hope she hasn't prepared anything too elaborate, he
thought as they drove away; it's very thoughtful of her to see
to the picnic like this, and no doubt it's her way of saying
thank you, as Mrs. Merry suggested, but I wouldn't want
her to go to a lot of expense.

It seemed that Clement Horder simply had to worry about
something or other in connection with this little outing.
There was no way in which he could relax and enjoy the
company of the woman with Angela's face who had, rather
to his surprise, turned out to be an honest and sensible sort
of person.

They drove in silence along suburban roads and then out
into the country. He had explained about his need to
concentrate and she had understood immediately, promising
she would not speak at all and keeping to her promise. That
too was unusual. Most people, including even his own
family at times, forgot about his problem and made remarks
to him at inconvenient moments. At a spot high up on a
downland road he turned the car onto the verge so that they
could admire the view. Even then she did not speak until he
assured her that he was free to listen now. A most unusual
woman indeed.

Then she simply said: "It's lovely up here. Would it be
too far to come back here to have our tea after we've been
down to the river?"

Commonplace words. The sort of words that thousands
of wives or sweethearts might have uttered on similar
occasions. But Clement Horder felt them catch at his heart
and make the sun seem brighter and the hills seem greener
and the sky appear an even deeper blue.

Many years ago now, almost as if it was in another life,
blue eyes had looked at him and a happy woman's voice had
said: "What a lovely spot! Let's picnic here." Joy once fled
cannot return. That's what the poet said, and it was true. But
perhaps he had looked at things too bleakly; shut himself up
too tightly in his chamber of silence. If past joys could
never be recovered, what about new joys, lesser joys, placid
and peaceful joys?

Such as this present joy of sitting on a hilltop next to a pretty grey-haired woman who treated his disability with tact but without making any fuss; who made things easy for him, and who seemed to be enjoying this moment every bit as much as he was himself. There was no affectation, no false rapture, in her voice.

"It's lovely here. Let's come back here for tea."

It was the authentic voice of that fresh young green shoot of an Amy whom nobody had ever seen before, whose existence she herself had never suspected. For one precious hour on a glorious summer day this Amy had triumphed over the others, beaten down the false self and the crazy self and opened herself in the sunlight. For this Amy, too, the skies seemed very bright and the hills seemed very green, and there was no need to plot or pretend or do anything at all except just to be.

They got out of the car and stood side by side leaning on a gate.

"Look, there's a hang glider," said Clement Horder.

"Where? Oh yes. I can see now. Oh, mustn't it be fun!"

The old false Amy would have shuddered delicately at the danger. The wild crazy Amy would have felt herself soar with the bird-man, contemptuously free of all the feeble earthbound things below. The new green shoot of an Amy simply saw a hang glider and said the first thing that came into her head to the man who had brought that young shoot into being.

How long did they stand there? Neither counted the minutes. Then time returned and simultaneously each gave the faintest of sighs and made a move back towards the car. That moment had gone, but there might be others.

"Now," said Clement as he switched on the engine, "I am afraid I must once again become incommunicado."

Amy raised her hand in a little mock salute. They smiled at each other. Oh yes, most certainly there were going to be other moments.

The wheels of the car were already turning when Clement Horder remembered that he had still not mentioned the important topic. Once they got down to botanising he would

go and forget it yet again. That wretched balcony. She'd
been out again last night, apparently totally unaware of its
dangers. He had every right to point them out to her, now
that they were truly friends. She would not think he was
being interfering. It would be a sign of how much she had
come to matter to him, that he was so concerned for her
safety.

He switched off the engine. Amy looked at him enquir-
ingly. Was there something wrong with the car?

"I've got something to say to you," he said with a little
laugh. How easy it was, now that they were truly friends!
That wonderful moment had melted all his worries away.
"As a matter of fact, I'm going to scold you a little. I said I
hoped you would come to look on me as a friend, and a
friend has a right to protest when he sees someone not
taking good care of herself."

It was gracefully and tactfully done. The old false Amy
would have simpered and fluttered. The little green shoot of
an Amy would have said in a straightforward manner that it
was very careless of her and she would not do it again. But
as soon as the word "balcony" was uttered, the wild Amy
of the thunderstorm and the schemes of revenge surged into
life and swamped both the other Amys.

Clement Horder was a trifle disappointed in her reaction.
She said the right things, of course, but somehow they
didn't sound quite right. Perhaps he had shown his interest
in her a little too quickly. After all, a lady had the right to set
the pace.

Never mind. There were bound to be ups and downs in
the process of getting acquainted. It would be a pleasant
drive from now on, and when they got down to the river he
would try to find her some orchids, and then they would
certainly come back up on the downs for their picnic tea.

Clement Horder was by no means unhappy as he steered
the car down the wooded hillside towards the river. He was
concentrating on the road and he had not the slightest
suspicion of the turmoil and torment going on in the mind
and heart of the human being who was sitting beside him.

The old false Amy had died forever. There was no room

left for her now. It was the little green shoot of an Amy that did not want to die and could not give up without a struggle, although it knew that it was doomed.

But I like him, it was saying to the monstrous powerful Amy who was strangling it to death; I'm sure he likes me too and doesn't mean me any harm.

You fool! hissed the terrible Amy. Silly sentimental fool. He's seen you on the balcony. He knows what you did next door. He's only playing with you until the time comes to give you away. You've got to get rid of him now. At once. At the very first opportunity.

But we were so happy, cried the other voice. We were both so happy, looking at the view together just now. That was true. That was no pretence. That was true happiness.

It was all pretence, retorted terrible Amy. He's just kidding you along. Playing cat and mouse.

Clement Horder risked a quick sideways glance at his companion. She was looking out of the window, her face turned away from him.

"Pretty road, isn't it?" he said, breaking his rule.

"It's lovely."

He did not hear her, but out of the corner of his eye he caught the flash of a smile as she turned her head briefly towards him before looking out of the side window again. He was reassured. It was going to be all right. In fact, it was already all right. She was no chatterbox. She was simply enjoying the drive.

That's right, kid him along, said terrible Amy; but watch out every second until you see your chance.

The steering wheel? They were going round hairpin bends now, steadily and carefully, but a sudden swerve could send him into oncoming traffic or off the road into a tree. She imagined the crash. Its violence excited her. Like the thunderstorm. But she would not be a spectator, revelling in the drama. She would be killed or injured herself. More likely injured, perhaps seriously.

Couldn't she jump clear in time? No hope. Not here. Not at the speed they were going. But if the car was moving very slowly, slowly but irrevocably; a car moving downhill

slowly but out of control. That was the situation she needed,
and there was no need to despair. The afternoon was still
young.

Meanwhile she was going to have to put up a pretence,
because the relief of the drive would soon be over. They
were on level ground now and had turned off along a narrow
winding lane, leaving most of the traffic behind. It certainly
was a quiet corner of the country, and very pretty. Shady
trees and grassy banks full of wild flowers, and even—

"A rabbit!" cried Amy aloud, clapping her hands
together and leaning forward.

Clement Horder stopped the car to let the little creature
scuttled off the road to safety. He glanced at his companion.
The fresh green shoot of Amy had made a brief reappear-
ance in that one moment of pleased surprise.

He drove on again happily. He wasn't even worrying any
longer about leaving her in the car while he went to look for
orchids. She was natural and unaffected and didn't make a
fuss. She would do just what she wanted to do. Everything
would be easy and open and friendly.

"Here we are," he said, turning off the narrow lane into
an even narrower field track.

"So this is your very special place," said Amy looking
out at the lush meadow that sloped gently down to the river.

"This is my favourite botanising spot, and I'm going to
park here because if I drive further down the path it's liable
to be muddy and we'll get the wheels stuck."

"In that case I think I'd better stay here while you go
treasure hunting. I haven't got the right shoes on, and I'd
probably only get in your way. Unless I get out and pick
some of these daisies. I might do that. Ought I to lock the
car?"

"Not unless you're going right out of sight, but I'll leave
you the keys just in case," said Mr. Horder.

He pointed out the door key to Amy and she thanked him.

"I doubt if I'll move far, though," she added. "I'm
feeling lazy and this is a beautiful spot. I'll just sit and
watch you, I think. How far are you going?"

"Just down this path, and then there'll be a bit of

scrambling about at the end. The bank is quite steep, and they'll be growing very near the water."

"Is the river deep here?" Amy asked.

"Fairly deep," he replied. "It narrows, you see. As if it were flowing through a sort of ravine."

"Off you go then. Good luck to you. I'll look forward to having a gorgeous purple bouquet."

"You're quite happy here?"

"Very happy indeed."

"Not afraid to be alone? I'm not going far."

"Not at all afraid to be alone," said Amy. "I shall commune with nature. I don't believe there's another human being within miles."

"I don't believe there is." He smiled at her. "I'm switching off now."

She smiled and waved as he shut the car door, and she continued to smile as he moved off down the track.

While they had been sitting chatting she had worked out exactly what she must do. It was very simple, and because of his deafness there was very little risk about it. The worst that could happen would be that he would look around at a vital moment, but it was not very likely, because he was a man who acted with deliberation and concentrated on what he was doing. At this moment he was concentrating on walking down the track to the riverbank at the end.

Amy moved her foot across the car, wrapped a handkerchief round her fingers, and pushed the gearshift into neutral. Many years ago, before she had become Philip's treasured Amy, there had been a short period of rebellion against being Daddy's precious Amy who was never to do anything that might involve any risk, like driving a car or going sailing. There had actually been a young man who had encouraged this revolt. Amy had forgotten his name, but she had a dim memory of an occasion when she had played truant instead of going to the secretarial college, and she actually drove his car quite a long way along a country road, without being authorised, but quite efficiently. The young man had called her a good sport and said she would soon be whizzing about on her own.

Memory failed as to what had happened next. Philip had

never wanted her to learn to drive, and Philip's Amy had never wanted to. But the Amy who was now about to use a car as a lethal weapon was diverted by the flash of memory into a sudden yearning to switch on the engine—the ignition key was still in place—reverse the car up to the road, and drive away, anywhere, on and on, all by herself.

No point in switching on the engine, said the cold practical Amy who for the second time was carrying out a murder. I'll have to leave it in neutral and use the slope of the hill. A stone under the wheel was the next thing. This little one would do. Just to hold the car back long enough for her to lean over and release the handbrake, and then move back and close the door.

Where had he got to? She was crouching behind the car now, out of sight of the man on the riverbank. But perhaps she had better show herself, just in case he looked around.

Amy stood up and came round to the side of the car. It seemed to be quivering as if about to move, and she reinforced the little stone with her foot. Clement Horder was near the water's edge. As she stood staring, with her hand shading her eyes against the sun, he turned round and waved. She waved back and then pointed at the long grass beside the track. It was dotted with white daisies. He seemed to nod, though it was difficult, against the sun and at this distance, to be quite sure of his movements, and then he turned round again and bent over to inspect a plant growing on the bank.

Amy kicked at the stone and drew her foot back, very quickly but not quite quickly enough to save it from being bruised by the moving wheel. She ought to have found a stick to push the stone away, but it would have taken time, and seconds were precious now.

The car moved at greater speed than she had expected and then came to a halt. Oh, that mud!

Amy limped after the car as quickly as she could and gave it a push. It moved again, gathering speed on the steeper incline to the water's edge. The man on the riverbank was still bending over his plants. He would not hear a thing. The car was coming straight at him. At any moment now.

Amy heard somebody cry out in a sort of strangled scream and then realized that she herself had made the sound. She began to run down the track. Her bruised foot slowed her progress. Her sight seemed to be failing too. She brushed a hand across her eyes and drew it away wet with tears.

"But I don't want him to die!"

The voice sounded clear and firm inside her head. She did not know whether she had spoken aloud. She could no longer see the figure at the water's edge. All she could see, and that only dimly, was the rutted earth on which she ran and the pale green back of the car, with the glass and the chromium winking in the bright sunlight.

"I don't want him to die, oh God, I don't want him to die!"

The voice went on and on. The bruised foot struggled and struggled. The glittering metal went ever faster. It was like a nightmare without end. And then suddenly her foot gave way and she was flat on her face on the earth. If felt cool and comforting. She shut her eyes. She did not want to move.

It seemed a long time that she lay there, and when the loud noise came she did not at first know what could have caused it. A rushing, tearing sort of noise; and a splashing, and somewhere there was something that could have been a human voice. Reluctantly she pulled herself up from the cool and pleasant earth, crouched on all fours like an animal, and stared ahead.

The sun still glinted on chromium and on pale green metal, and sticking up above the edge of the bank were two back wheels of the car. One of them seemed to be caught in a tuft of thick grass. Even as she stared, it released itself and both wheels sank lower.

Amy got to her feet and limped forward. The car was tilted right over the bank, its nose buried in the mud at the side of the river. There was no sign of a human being.

She looked up and down the river. Had he miraculously got clear in time? Had he swum away? The thought brought a little surge of hope which was quickly wiped out by despair. That was no use. He would know she had tried to murder him.

But he couldn't have swum away. The river was clear in both directions. If he had swum at all he would have climbed out again as soon as possible.

Then where was he? Hiding behind that hedge, waiting to jump out on her? Or up on the road, waiting for a passing car to take him to fetch the police?

That was what it was, of course. She must have stayed longer than she realised, lying on that welcoming earth. Perhaps she had lost consciousness. Any minute now they would come for her and it would be useless to plead that she hadn't meant to try to kill him and that he was her friend.

"I didn't do it!" she cried aloud to the silently accusing summer landscape. "It wasn't me! It wasn't me, not me, not me . . ."

She began to walk again, no longer noticing the pain in her foot.

"It wasn't me, wasn't me, wasn't me . . ."

When she came to the upturned car she hit at the muddy rubber of the wheel with both hands and her mutterings rose to a shriek.

"It wasn't me! Wasn't me!"

She fell forward over the wheel, breathless and exhausted. It seemed to shift a little beneath her weight, and in her ears there was a sound of creaking and straining, as if something was trying to move, trying to escape.

"It's your fault! You did it!" cried Amy, thumping at the wheel with all her strength.

It shifted sideways, and then suddenly made a big movement, and she was lying straddled over the wheel of the car, her feet no longer on the earth, and her eyes looking down upon dark muddy water.

Her mind was as blank and clouded as the river. It seemed that there was something floating just beneath the surface, something very big and solid and important, but she could not understand what it was. She could not reach that thing lying in the thick dark water. Her eyes closed. The sun was burning upon her back. The bed on which she lay was hard and uncomfortable. Perhaps she could get into the car: that would give her shade.

She wriggled around on the side of the car. It shook a little but made no big movement. After a while she felt the door handle. It took a very long time to pull the door upwards but she persisted, very slowly, very patiently, with little clawing movements like a cat.

At last it opened and she pulled it right back and slid down into the interior, holding tight to the tilted seats and the steering wheel. It felt damp and cool inside. She kicked off her shoes. Her feet were in water, cool water. She propped herself against the tilted-up seat with her feet in the water and shut her eyes.

It was like a grave, an upright grave.

6

The inquest on Clement Horder was postponed for a while in the hope that the survivor of the accident might be well enough to give evidence in person, but in the end Mrs. Langford's statement had to be read in her absence. It looked as if she was going to remain in hospital for quite a long time. The shock and the pneumonia had not only seriously weakened her body, but seemed permanently to have disordered her mind.

For much of the time she lay motionless, with eyes open staring at nothing. When she did speak it made little sense.

"The bird-man," she muttered. And then: "Going back up the hill."

Jonathan Langford, telephoned in New York by a very worried London secretary, flew home at once without the least protest, and talked to Bob and Sue Merry for a while before going to the hospital.

"I never saw her that morning at all," said Sue. "Mr. Horder gave me her message about not being in for lunch."

Jonathan was inclined to bluster and to blame. All his life he had watched his mother's strangling ivy-like hold upon his father, and when at last the parasite had destroyed the

tree it clung to, he himself was determined not to be thus
stifled in his turn. He had no near relatives with whom to
share the burden. His father's friends, enduring Amy for the
sake of poor Philip, drifted away as soon as they decently
could; and Jonathan's own friends produced plenty of
sympathy but kept a safe distance.

And so he had had to make his stand alone. The right
wife might have helped, but although there had been plenty
of women in Jonathan's life, he had never married. He
always told his friends that the example of his parents had
put him off forever, but to himself he was more honest. He
had been unable to find the courage either to introduce the
girl he loved to his mother or to marry without telling his
mother, and in the end his girl had given up and left him.
The grief at his loss and the shame of his own weakness
combined to fan the flames of his hatred and resentment of
his mother when the moment came when he had to fight or
go under. The memory of that scene was no less painful to
him than it was to Amy. It had to be brutal, but so great was
his own fear of weakening that he had made it doubly so.
The guilt that followed had been torturing, nagging at him
ceaselessly, wherever he was, whatever he was doing.
There were times when Jonathan Langford wondered
whether it had been worth it. Surely not even his mother's
stranglehold could have been worse than this feeling of
having stabbed right into the very core of a human creature,
tearing away every single shred of the protective self-
deception by which alone the human creature can survive.

It was an appalling thing to do to anybody, let alone one's
own mother. Had she been a different sort of person, he
might even have been responsible for a suicide. But she
quickly picked up her self-deceptive illusions again, for she
was, after all, an adept at cushioning herself in this manner.
In fact, she consisted almost entirely of such illusions. She
had no other character, except perhaps a tiny kernel of truth
somewhere that was so frail and unformed that it had no
hope of ever growing.

But perhaps it could have grown a little if Jonathan had
been patient and tried to tend it instead of running away

after he had won his battle, for fear he would have to battle yet again.

Guilt gnawed at him. Letters from his friend who was Chairman of the Digby Hall Committee, telling him that his mother seemed to have settled in quite happily, did nothing to ease his mind. Amy herself sent nothing except a few picture postcards with comments about the weather. Jonathan would have felt less bad if she had written him long letters of reproach, telling him how miserable she was to be living there.

He knew he ought to go and visit her. For Amy Langford the outward show was everything. It was vital to her that the other people at Digby Hall should see that she was visited and taken out by her son. Several times he nearly drove down to the coast, but always at the last moment his courage failed him. Suppose she really was bitterly unhappy. Suppose she should beg him pitifully to take her away? How on earth would he be able to resist, with this great burden of guilt weakening him? How often had he watched his father struggle in vain against the paralysing suckers of this monstrous parasite that had given Jonathan his life!

And so Jonathan Langford put it off and put it off, and as his life was full and active, the time sped by, and the more he put it off the less was he able to face doing it. Once he had telephoned, and found his mother out, and Mrs. Merry had answered him that Mrs. Langford was well, enjoying the garden in this lovely weather, and making friends with the other residents. Jonathan had pretended to himself that it was good for his mother to have a greater variety of company. They seemed to be a nice lot at Digby Hall; perhaps she might yet turn into a better and a happier person.

The news of the accident came as a slashing blow. To think that it might be in any way due to his own neglect was intolerable. There must be somebody else at fault, somebody else to blame. Only if he could find some sort of inefficiency or slackness at Digby Hall would he feel better. He picked on the fact that the young warden had not actually seen his mother on the day of the disaster.

"But surely you check up on everybody every morning,"
he said to Sue Merry. "It's not as if you've got dozens of
residents. There's only a few of them. It can't be too
onerous a task to make sure they are all right."

"I do if they ask me," replied Sue faintly. "Some of
them prefer to be left alone."

She could say no more. Her nerves were stretched to
breaking point, even with the tranquillisers that Dr. Cunningham had given her. First Mrs. Graham, and then this
terrible business of Mr. Horder and Mrs. Langford. Not
that anybody had blamed her up till now, not even Mrs.
Gurney. In fact, all the Committee members, though deeply
shocked, had gone out of their way to comfort and reassure
Sue Merry. Feuds had been forgotten. Digby Hall had
closed ranks against the world.

Sue had support from them all. All except her own
husband. Bob was impatient with her nerves, thought she
was being too sensitive, making too much fuss. Of course it
was a very great pity about old Horder. Bob had always
liked him. And of course all these enquiries were a great
nuisance. But it would all get sorted out eventually.
Meanwhile it was miserable for everybody. There was no
reason why Sue should feel it more than anybody else.

Bob Merry was a caring and kindhearted man, but he did
not want to realise how much he depended on his wife. It
hurt his young pride that Sue did not seem to find his love
and support enough to help her through this present crisis.
He felt that it ought to be enough. There was tension
between them. Their relationship had never been strained in
this way before.

"Had my mother specially asked to be left alone?"
demanded Jonathan Langford.

Sue shook her head.

"Then I think you could have made some attempt to let
her feel that somebody cared about her," said Jonathan.

Sue bit her lip. She could not speak.

Bob answered for her, annoyed that she let herself be
bullied like this. "Both my wife and I have given your
mother every possible care and attention, Mr. Langford. If

we'd done any more we should have been intruding. If you've got any complaints about us, they should be made to the Committee. They make all the decisions and we carry them out."

"There's such a thing as using intelligent judgement," snapped Jonathan.

"My wife and I are always exercising our judgement," retorted Bob.

Sue put a hand on his arm. He shook it off impatiently. "If you really thought your mother was not being properly looked after here, there was nothing to stop you coming to check up for yourself."

Jonathan drew in his breath sharply. He was much the same height and build as Bob Merry, but some ten or twelve years older. For a moment they stood glaring at each other in silence. Sue wrung her hands together to try to stop their trembling. Then Jonathan said icily: "I cannot imagine that being offensive to the relatives of residents is included among your responsibilities. I shall speak to the Chairman of the Committee. Now perhaps you will kindly direct me to the hospital."

Bob accompanied him to his car and Sue ran straight to Dr. Cunningham's flat. He produced an even stronger tranquilliser and sat talking to her for a long time. When she had calmed down enough to go, he sat on alone, looking very thoughtful and very worried. Something was going to have to be done, and done quickly, if yet another tragedy at Digby Hall was to be prevented.

"Mother, it's me. It's me. Jonathan."

The head shifted slightly on the pillows. The blue eyes stared at him blankly.

"Don't you know me, Mother? Can't you see me?"

The eyes closed for a moment, then opened and stared again.

"I came at once when I heard," said Jonathan. "I dropped everything and flew home at once."

Was there a change of expression? Certainly there seemed to be a slight movement of the lips. Jonathan leant forward. It was almost as if—no, surely it could not be?—it was almost as if she was sneering at him.

But she had never sneered at anybody; that had never been her way. It must be due to her illness, to the weakness after the fever. Or perhaps she was still delirious. She seemed to be trying to talk. He leant forward again and just caught the murmured words.

"We were to be friends."

"You and this Mr.—?" Jonathan found he had forgotten the dead man's name.

"Perhaps get married."

The voice was lower than ever; the eyelids drooped and remained closed.

Good lord, said Jonathan to himself, leaning back in the chair. Married! Well, why not? Such things were not unknown in old people's homes. And his mother was certainly well-groomed and elegant and superficially agreeable if she thought it worth her while. So she'd been working on this poor old boy—damn it, what *was* his name? Friends. Going to get married.

Jonathan smiled to himself, his good temper quite restored. That was quick work on his mother's part. You had to hand it to her, she really could hook a man. And once hooked—but better not think about that now. After all, the poor man was dead. Extraordinary thing, that. One of those inexplicable accidents. Brake failure, most likely. Cars did sometimes start rolling downhill of their own accord. Pity, though. Might even have turned out quite well if his mother had married this man.

A great pity. For wasn't that exactly what Jonathan had hoped for her, after his father died? That she would meet someone else who could take care of her as she needed to be cared for? And incidentally relieve Jonathan of the burden. Even if it hadn't turned out well; even if this unknown dead man had come deeply to regret the marriage, it would still have relieved Jonathan of his burden.

In fact, in a sense it had already relieved him, just hearing his mother murmur those few words.

Friends. Going to be married.

The words echoed in Jonathan's mind like an absolution. His mother had made friends with a man whom she was going to marry. That meant she had been happy, had completely recovered from the terrible scene between them. There was no need for him to feel guilty at all. By forcing her to lead her own life he had in fact opened out a much wider life for her. He had positively done her a service.

A nurse came into the room and Jonathan had hastily to compose his features lest the joy and relief should appear insuitable in the circumstances.

"She seems a little better," he said. "She's actually been talking to me." And he told the nurse what his mother had said, making much of it.

She was suitably grieved. "How dreadful! Just when they had so much to look forward to."

Jonathan agreed.

"But it's a good thing she's told you that," went on the nurse. "It might help them in trying to find out what happened."

Jonathan agreed again. His mother's muttered words became more and more clear and firm every time he told the tale. Wonderful words, absolving him of guilt. He would most gladly and with a clear conscience stand up in any court in the land and swear that his mother had been spending a happy afternoon with the man whom she was going to marry.

Later on he arranged to meet Clement Horder's son and daughter-in-law and they all three grieved together over the sad fate of the elderly lovers.

"We always hoped my father would marry again," said Clement Horder's son, "but he never showed any sign of it up till now."

"And I always hoped my mother would," said Jonathan.

They expressed sympathy to each other.

"Is she able to tell at all what happened?" asked Clement's son.

"Not yet, I'm afraid. There seems to be complete blockage. She remembers the drive and turning into the meadow where your father was going to pick flowers, but she becomes very distressed and quite incoherent if asked any questions about what happened next."

"It's a shame they have to bother her. As if she hasn't been through enough." It was the daughter-in-law speaking.

"Well, I suppose they've got to try and find out," said Jonathan reasonably.

"Poor old Dad," said Clement's son sadly. "But it's a comfort to know that his last hours must have been happy. Of course it would be more satisfactory to know exactly what did happen, but it won't bring him back, and since there's no question of blaming anybody, I really rather hope they won't persist too long in these enquiries. I certainly don't think your mother should have to be distressed any more about it."

The authorities appeared to share this view. As the newspaper reports of the tragedy said, "Police do not suspect foul play."

Death was due to drowning. Bruises found on the body could have been caused by its bumping about in the car as the vehicle tipped over the edge into the river, and by the descending falling through the door of the driver's seat, which must have burst open with the impact, into the water. There had been a knock on his head which might have caused unconsciousness. There was no sign of any heart disease, nor any other disorder that could have led to fainting fits or blackouts. Apart from the deafness, deceased was in fair condition for a man of his age.

Ferrier's Motor Company representative stated that the car was in good condition too. It had been serviced only the previous week. Mr. Horder had hired that very car twice before. His driving licence was in order; the company knew him to be a reliable customer and a careful driver, though it was agreed that the deafness could be a problem.

Suicide was quickly disposed of. Several people stated that Clement Horder always appeared to be contented with his life, in no way disturbed or depressed. Sue Merry, looking very disturbed and depressed herself, told of her last conversation with him. She was listened to with interest. She was, after all, the last person to have had anything like a personal conversation with Mr. Horder, since he had sat in his usual silence throughout the midday meal before he left Digby Hall for the last time.

Mrs. Merry stated that he seemed to be looking forward to his afternoon's outing. A little concerned about where to go for tea. That was all. Men did not drown themselves as well as their chosen companions, because they were not sure where to go for tea. Of the two other people who had spoken to Mr. Horder after that last meal, the man at the garage who had handed the car over confirmed that the deceased had seemed cheerful and contented; and the woman who was—presumably—the last person to see him alive was unable to give evidence. No doubt she would have stated that he was cheerful and contented too, as well as he might have been, if they had just got engaged to be married. But as far as giving any clue to the cause of the accident was concerned, why, she might just as well have drowned too, as indeed she very nearly had.

The most informative statement of the lot came from the man who had rescued her. John Willett, retired engineer, was driving his Land-Rover along the quiet country lane on his way to look at a small farmhouse that he was thinking of buying. He had been going slowly, taking an interest in his surroundings, and that was how he had noticed what was at the end of the field track that led down to the river.

His first thought was it was a stolen and abandoned car, such as one sometimes saw at the roadside or on a bit of wasteland. The track was only gently sloping. One could easily jump out while the car was moving and leave it to go on its way. Or give it a push to help it along.

Such had been Mr. Willett's train of thought as he drove his Land-Rover down the field path, most effectively obliterating the tracks of the other vehicle that had passed that way. He had certainly not expected to find a human being on the scene. It came as quite a shock to see the body in the car; or rather, what he thought at the time was the body in the car. Mr. Willett was a lively, voluble person, and had quite a gift for dramatic description.

The body of the woman whom he later learnt was Mrs. Amy Langford, now living in a sort of twilight world of the mind, was propped up against the front seat of the car with its legs entwined in the steering wheel. The car, you see, was lying on its side, explained Mr. Willett, and was gradually sinking deeper into the mud and shifting away from the bank.

He explained in detail how he had climbed onto it, thus causing it to shift still more under his weight, and the great difficulty he had had in extracting the body from the half-submerged car. She was a dead weight. He would probably have abandoned the struggle and driven off to get help if he had not discovered that the woman was in fact alive.

When he finally got her on to land she actually opened her eyes but didn't seem to see anything. Breathing and heartbeats appeared to be reasonably all right, and he thought there might be internal injuries or broken bones; certainly some concussion. He debated for a moment about driving her to a hospital himself, but decided it was better left to the experts. The bumpy Land-Rover might just finish her off. So he got out a groundsheet and a rug and made her as comfortable as he could, then drove quickly to the nearest telephone box.

While waiting at the scene of action for the ambulance and police to arrive, Mr. Willett did a little more detective work and came to the conclusion that the woman had been trying to climb out of the car when she succumbed to whatever injury or illness had overtaken her. He also began to wonder whether she had been alone in the car. There was not, as far as he could see, any sign that somebody had drowned in the river, but it was the driver's side of the car that was now deep in the water.

The woman might have been the passenger, saved because her side was uppermost. And that meant, continued Mr. Willet, his lively litle nut-like face crinkling with remembered horror, that there might well be a body trapped in the water underneath the car.

Mr. Willett was right in that conclusion at least. When the lifting gear had done its work and the pale green Cortina

was retrieved from its muddy bed, there really was a body
that had been trapped underneath the car. Also retrieved
from the car was a picnic basket, a thermos flask, and some
dirty wet plastic bags containing what must have once been
some tasty savouries and cakes.

What had caused the accident? Why should a happy
summer afternoon's excursion come to such a tragic end?
Nobody would ever know. Unless perhaps one day some
dim memory should stir in the mercifully blank mind of the
survivor. But who could wish for that? The poor woman had
suffered enough. A nice woman, by all accounts. A widow
conquering her own grief and looking forward to a little late
happiness. Two lonely people coming together to comfort
each other. One was now beyond all comfort; the other
hovered in a no-man's-land, withdrawn into some secret
world of her own.

"What do the doctors think about your mother?" said
Clement Horder's son to Jonathan when the inquest was
over. He felt sorry for Jonathan Langford. It was better to
have a parent dead, genuinely mourned but definitely dead,
than to have a parent in this half-alive condition.

"They don't know what to make of her," replied
Jonathan. He looked worried, because he had quite a
problem on his hands, but his intolerable burden of guilt
was gone forever, and he could cope with any other
problem. "She's getting stronger physically," he went on,
"but seems as confused in mind as ever. I think I've
probably got to face it, that she's never going to be able to
look after herself again. Not even in sheltered accommodation."

He received murmurs of sympathy.

"Of course the hospital can't keep her much longer," he
said. "I'm investigating nursing homes."

"That's going to cost something."

"It is indeed, but I can't see any alternative. Unless—"
Jonathan paused a moment and looked thoughtful. "If only
I could arrange for proper nursing care, I don't see why she
shouldn't go back to Digby Hall."

"Oh. Do you think that's wise? Wouldn't she prefer to forget it?"

"She has forgotten it," said Jonathan bluntly. "Or rather she's forgotten all the unpleasantness connected with it. In one of her clearer moments she was talking about the sun terrace and her seat in the shrubbery. I've a feeling she might like to be there. But the nursing is a problem. That girl they've got there is no good."

His listeners jumped to Mrs. Merry's defence. She was not meant to be nursing the residents. It was actually meant to be a part-time job, but she gave much more of her time and effort than she was supposed to.

Jonathan hastily changed his tune. There was no point in trying to show that Mrs. Merry had been neglectful. After all, he was quite free of his own burden of guilt now, and had no need to shift it onto another. The more he thought about getting his mother back to Digby Hall, the better he liked the idea. It would save him no end of trouble. Probably a bit of expense as well. He would talk to his friend who was Chairman of the Committee. They had two empty flats there now, and were apparently having some difficulty in filling them. Gone were the days when Mr. Fisher and Mrs. Gurney did battle over who was to have the privilege of being offered an apartment.

Digby Hall was under a cloud. Two residents had died, one in a tragic and mysterious way. A third seemed to be marred for life. People didn't like that sort of thing. They would keep their names on the waiting list and wait to see how things turned out, but they wouldn't be all that keen to rush in at this juncture. Suppose his mother were to return to her flat, with a nurse-companion installed in the flat next door? She could be offered the apartment free, or at a small rent, and he, Jonathan Langford, would of course pay her a salary for looking after his mother. They didn't need to join in the communal life. Each flat had its own kitchen and bathroom. They could keep strictly to themselves.

Yes, this was an excellent idea. He would put it forward at once. It would be just the job for one of the many lonely and impoverished widows with a little home nursing experience. Just the job. Those sticklers for the letter of the law would make a fuss on the Committee, but Jonathan Langford had no doubt of being able to carry the day. He was a man with a grievance. He had put his mother into their care, trusting that she would be safe and happy there, and look what had happened to her!

Even if no one person could ever be held to blame, nobody could deny that Jonathan Langford had every reason to feel aggrieved.

About a week after the inquest on Clement Horder, Dr. George Cunningham interrupted a slow-moving and lacklustre game of chess to say: "I'm sorry, Nancy. My mind's not on it. I can't stop thinking about that child."

Miss Pick knew instantly who "that child" was.

"Don't you think Sue will be better now that all the enquiries have stopped?" she asked.

"She might have been," was the grim reply, "if it hadn't been for this crazy idea of bringing Mrs. Langford back here."

"It is a crazy idea," agreed Nancy, "but surely it won't come to anything, not with Mr. Fisher and Mrs. Gurney both against it."

"It oughtn't to, but young Langford is as obstinate as the devil. And as bloody-minded, and he's put the fear of God into the Chairman. I wouldn't put it past him to start spreading rumours about this place just to get his own way."

"Oh dear," said Nancy Pick inadequately.

"And any hint of mismanagement or neglect is just what we can do without just now," went on George Cunningham.

He turned back to the chessboard and made another desultory move. "It's no good, Nancy," he went on. "I've just got to go and see if young Sue is all right. Coming?"

"Certainly."

They were playing chess in his flat on the gound floor. On the way upstairs Nancy Pick said: "It's a pity she has to be alone in the evenings when Bob's at his class."

"H'm. Yes, I suppose so. Not that young Merry seems to be going the right way to help her. The girl needs to talk it over and over, not to be constantly told to forget it."

"Why do you think Sue is so upset?" asked Nancy. "She's not in the least to blame."

"Not in the least. But someone is trying to make her think she is."

"But who?" persisted Nancy as they walked along the landing to the door of the warden's flat. "Bob wouldn't be doing that to her, and there's no one else here now, except you and me. And Mrs. Ramsden," she added as an afterthought. "I'd almost forgotten her. One sees so little of her nowadays. What is she doing with herself?"

"Drinking," said Dr. Cunningham abruptly. "When she's not nagging at Sue."

They knocked at the door. There was no reply.

"Well, Mrs. Ramsden can't be in with her now," said Nancy, "or she'd come to the door."

George Cunningham looked very worried. "I don't like this. I think we'll have to go in and investigate. I'll have to confess to you, Nancy, that I arranged with Mrs. Gurney to have another master key." He was turning it in the lock as he spoke. "Don't tell anyone else. Sue and Bob don't know. I wouldn't dream of using it except in emergency."

The lights in the sitting room of the warden's flat were on but there was nobody there. Nor in the bedroom, nor the kitchen. The bathroom door was shut and seemed to be bolted. There was dead silence in the flat. Then there came the sound of steadily running water. The two people standing outside the white door stared at each other, and for a moment it was the man who looked the more reassured.

"If she's just having a bath," he said softly, "then of course there's no need to interfere. But I'd rather feared—"

He left the sentence unfinished.

"You thought she'd swallowed too many pills," said Nancy Pick. "I still think we ought to check."

She knocked sharply on the bathroom door. "Mrs. Merry. Sue!" she cried, raising her voice to be heard above the sound of running water.

There was no response. She knocked and shouted again. "It's only me. Nancy. There's nothing wrong. I just wanted to talk to you."

Still no reply. "But she must hear, she *must,*" said George Cunningham.

Again they stared at each other. "If it's like all the other flats it'll only be a very flimsy bolt," said Nancy Pick.

"All right. If we're making fools of ourselves it'll have been worth it."

They put their combined weights against the door. It gave a little. They tried again, and presently there was the sound of rending wood.

Nancy Pick was the first to step inside, and the first thing she saw was the black hair showing up against the white of the bathtub. It showed so clearly because the girl was lying face downwards, submerged in the water except for the floating hair. Both taps were turned on full; the bath was filling rapidly. Dr. Cunningham turned off the taps while Nancy Pick raised the girl from the water. Between them they wrapped towels round her, carried her to the bed.

Some time later, seated by the still unconscious girl, Dr. Cunningham said: "It's a good thing we weren't five minutes later."

Nancy glanced at the half-empty bottle of tablets that he was holding.

"She'll sleep them off," he said. "It wasn't a fatal dose. But left much longer, she'd have drowned."

"Making doubly sure?"

"Could be. Or genuine mental confusion from the drug."

For a few minutes they remained silent, the heavy, red-faced man and the angular, straggle-haired woman, looking at the girl on the bed. A young and pretty girl, bright and lively, caring and compassionate. A good and lovable young life. The two people staring at her were growing old and had never been beautiful. They had both led useful lives and many people had been grateful for their services, but neither had ever aroused deep devotion in another human creature's heart. George Cunningham had once had a wife who had deserted him, and he knew very well that any interest Mrs. Gurney might have in him was not for any charm of his own but because she wanted the status of a married woman again. Nancy Pick had once loved very deeply and had known the pain of rejection.

Two old people without much to look forward to, and yet their will to live was stronger than that of the young one who had everything. They stared with painful tenderness at the life that they had saved, and then, both moved by the same thoughts, they looked at each other and both spoke the same words at the same moment.

"Nobody else must know."

"She won't wake for hours," said George, "and she won't remember much of what happened when she does."

"So Bob can think she's just asleep," said Nancy.

Then once again they both exclaimed together: "The bathroom door!"

"Damn. That's a giveaway," said Nancy.

They both thought hard.

"I suppose we couldn't possibly mend it before Bob gets back?" she said at last.

"Not a chance. In fact, we ought to be going now. We'll just have to leave it. Let him worry about it and wonder what's happened," added George as he got to his feet. "Serve him right for not taking better care of Sue. And I'll have a long talk with her in the morning. This is not going to happen again." His flushed face was grim. "There've been too many deaths at Digby Hall."

"Too many deaths at Digby Hall," said Nancy when they were once more seated in his apartment with the unfinished chess game between them. "It frightens me, George, and I'm not easily scared. Mrs. Graham dies, Mr. Horder dies,

Mrs. Langford nearly dies, and Sue Merry tries to kill herself and nearly dies. It's like one of those thrillers where somebody is doing away with a whole household, one by one. That sounds awfully silly,'' added the sensible Miss Pick with a nervous little laugh quite unlike her usual unladylike guffaw.

George Cunningham did not laugh at all. "A whole household," he repeated thoughtfully. "Yes, it certainly does look as if the Fates have got a grudge against Digby Hall."

"Of course I didn't really mean," began Nancy, and then stopped.

What had she not really meant? She was a very honest woman and at this moment she was very troubled. They sat in two shabby but comfortable armchairs, with the chess-board on a plain wooden coffee table between them. A standard lamp with a yellowish parchment shade gave them ample light. In the shadows beyond its range were the divan bed in the alcove, the crimson curtains with their faded patches, the mahogany chest and bookcase, the Persian carpet that was too big even for this spacious room and was turned under at the window side. When Dr. Cunningham had been living in the rather smaller apartment above, before he changed over with Mrs. Graham, the carpet had required an even wider fold.

Nancy looked at all these familiar things but they failed to bring her the usual comfort. She really had meant what she said. It seemed to her that there was some terrible doom overhanging Digby Hall. Not even this pleasant homely room was exempt from the sense of—well, she supposed one would have to call it evil, although she had always maintained there was no such thing as evil, and that everything could be excused or explained. George Cunningham held much the same view. They sometimes varied their chess evenings by a little philosophical discussion, lending each other books and commenting on them.

If she were to say aloud what she was really thinking now, George would think she had gone crazy, and that would be intolerable to Nancy, because their well-defined

companionship meant a lot to her. But it had already begun
to change its nature after the death of Mrs. Graham, and this
evening had changed it almost out of recognition. The
rescuing of Sue Merry had stirred up the very deepest
feelings about life and death, hope and belief. It was
impossible to slip easily back into a shared intellectual
exercise.

George Cunningham's thoughts had been running along
much the same lines, but he had always been more willing
than Nancy was to believe in the existence of evil. Years in
medical practice made it less easy to ignore than did years
of teaching intelligent pupils. But he had always rather
played down his own feelings when talking to Nancy. Their
companionship meant a great deal to him too, but she gave
the impression of being a very "no nonsense" sort of
person, and he did not want to spoil their contentment by
revealing that he himself was really rather an emotional
person under the surface. But the situation at Digby Hall
was becoming too alarming to allow for such minor worries;
he had thoughts about it that he could not possibly share
with Mrs. Gurney or any other of the Committee, but he
could share them with Nancy.

"I believe you're thinking what I am," he said firmly,
"that we've got a problem here that's a lot stickier than any
chess problem we've ever come across. We'll have to put
our heads together, Nan, and try a spot of detective work for
a change."

It struck just the right note. They were happy together
again. George made coffee and they talked for some time.

"So it boils down to this," said Nancy. "On the facts as
we know them, there is one common factor in these
tragedies. Sue Merry was the last person to see Mrs.
Graham alive and it was she who found her dead. Of those
at Digby Hall, Sue Merry was the last to see Mrs. Langford
before the accident, and she was the last person to have any
conversation with Mr. Horder. And tonight Sue Merry
nearly succeeded in killing herself. Unless you think there
might have been somebody else involved?"

George began to shake his head and then suddenly
stopped. "The bolt on the bathroom door," he said.

"But there's a window. Quite a big one for a bathroom. And it looks out over the roof of the garage."

They stared at each other. Then George said: "I don't believe anybody tried to kill Sue Merry."

"Neither do I. I'm only pointing out that it would not be impossible to get into the bathroom of the warden's flat from outside. But the window was shut, wasn't it?"

George thought for a moment. "Yes. Tight shut. To get in from outside would be very difficult. But when Bob starts making enquiries about the broken bolt, there'll be no harm in pointing out the possibility. It'll do him good to worry about Sue a bit more."

"You don't think Bob himself—"

"Killed Mrs. Graham and pushed Mr. Horder and Mrs. Langford into the river and then tried to kill his wife because she'd guessed? Why on earth should he? He's perfectly sane. And a very decent young man for the most part."

"I admit that the theory does rather belong to the realms of fiction," said Nancy, "but if we are going on the assumption that there is a human hand and mind that is in some way responsible for these events, then we have to face the fact that that hand and mind belong to somebody who on the surface appears perfectly sane and decent. Or at any rate, perfectly respectable. Not a raving maniac or an obvious villain."

George leant forward in his chair and made her a little bow. "Madam, I sit corrected. You are perfectly right. Nobody can be eliminated. Not even you and me."

Nancy laughed in her old unaffected way. The Amy Langford who had come to Digby Hall would have thought: What a frightful woman! Just like a horse! George Cunningham, for all his deep and genuine concern for the young Merrys and for Digby Hall, looked at Nancy laughing and felt a glow at the heart such as he had not experienced for many years.

"All right then," he said, joining in. "Let's investigate you and me."

He produced a calendar and they checked dates and tried

to recall their own actions at specified times. The conversation, which started by being very methodical and quite serious, became more and more frivolous and lighthearted.

"You are a much more likely person than me," said Nancy. "Doctors are always good suspects. Access to poisons and anatomical knowledge and all that sort of thing. Obviously, you popped a fatal pill into poor Mrs. Graham's bottle of heart tablets."

"And equally obviously, it was you who tampered with the car that ran into the river. Plenty of people would swear to your mechanical expertise."

"How did I fix the brakes to fail at that particular moment?"

"I haven't the faintest idea," said George cheerfully. "My anatomical knowledge doesn't extend to the automobile. How about you telling me how you did it?"

"How about us both looking for a motive? Mrs. Graham—mercy killing is all I can think of. Mr. Horder?"

"Sorry. Can't think of a motive at all. I liked Horder," added George Cunningham with the hint of a return to seriousness.

"So did I." Nancy echoed his change of tone. "But I could cheerfully have murdered Mrs. Langford," she continued. "Anytime. Couldn't stand the woman. Moment I set eyes on her, I thought, here's a female egoist if ever there was one. Doing the helpless little woman act to get her own way."

"She certainly isn't a type to appeal to other women," said George more mildly.

"But to men?"

"You know my opinion of her, my dear. Very much the same as yours. But evidently Clement Horder felt differently."

"Unless he tried to get rid of her and it backfired."

"Why should he try to get rid of her?" demanded George.

"I don't know," she admitted. "I suppose the police really have done their best to find out what happened."

"Seems so." George was suddenly gloomy. "Damn it,

there's so little to go on. Just this vague feeling that something is very wrong, some malevolent force at work. The more we talk, the stronger it gets. You too?"

"Me too. Look here, if we haven't any facts, let's tackle it from the psychological angle. Let's look for examples of malevolence. Who is there connected with Digby Hall who is actually capable of scheming to make somebody else suffer?"

"Good idea, Nan. That rules you out at once."

"Thank you. You too."

"And Mrs. Graham, bless her soul."

"And Mr. Horder."

"Sue Merry certainly. Bob too. There's no ill will in him. He's just not being very sensible about a very nervous wife."

"We're disposing of people very quickly," said Nancy. "What about the Committee members?"

"Sorry to disappoint you," said George after a moment's thought, "but I can't think of any member of the Committee who would be a suitable suspect from the psychological angle. Stupid, yes. Obstinate, yes. Infuriating, yes. But capable of maliciously plotting harm to another creature— no, I'm afraid the answer is no. Not even our local Lady Bountiful, Theodora Gurney."

"I agree with you," said Nancy. "Bossiness and inter-feringness are very disagreeable qualities, but they are not the ones we are looking for. It's someone who looks different from what they really are that we want. An underground operator."

"I suppose you realise," countered George, "that in our survey of possible ill-wishers, we have eliminated all the names except two."

"I do indeed. Mrs. Langford and Mrs. Ramsden."

"Mrs. Langford herself very nearly died, and it is by no means certain that she will ever live a normal life again," said George in a rather forced manner.

"She can't be eliminated on that count," said Nancy sharply. "Fictional murderers frequently contrive attempts on their own life to divert suspicion."

"Such as driving a car into a river and pushing the other person under before getting out just in time oneself?"

Nancy nodded.

"But as far as we know, Mrs. Langford can't drive," protested George.

"Maybe she suggested that Mr. Horder should give her a lesson. Quiet country road, field path right off the road. Ideal place for a beginner."

"It could make sense," said George slowly. "But look here, it was Sue Merry who felt driven past endurance tonight. Mrs. Langford is still in hospital. She certainly didn't put Sue in the bath. Or are you suggesting she engineered Sue's final collapse from her hospital bed?"

"She's in a private room," said Nancy, "and there's such a thing as the telephone."

"Good God. So there is. I hadn't thought of that." George jumped up from his chair, looking worried.

At the same moment the phone rang. They exchanged anxious looks as George lifted the receiver, and then Nancy relaxed a little when she heard him speak.

"Hullo, Bob. No, you're not disturbing me. It's chess night . . . a break-in? No, we've not heard anything . . . how very odd. And Sue is fast asleep, you say? . . . All right, I'll come across. No wonder you're worried. Shan't be a moment." He put the phone down and made a grimace. "Now I've got to do a bit of lying and pretending. Unless . . ."

"I think we ought to tell him the truth," said Nancy. "I know I said earlier that we should keep quiet to make it easier for Sue, but I've changed my mind since we've been talking. You said yourself that Mrs. Ramsden had been nagging at her, and if Mrs. Langford has been doing the same as well—"

"You're quite right. I'll tell Bob everything. Don't go away, Nan. I'll be back."

George Cunningham found a very worried young man in the warden's flat.

"It's quite crazy," burst out Bob the moment he appeared. "There's nothing missing and no other damage and no other sign of a break-in and Sue's fast asleep and I can't wake her, and why the hell should somebody go and bust in the bathroom door and nothing else, and how did they get in in any case? Honestly, Dr. Cunningham, this place is getting me down. It seems to have a jinx on it. I'm beginning to understand how Sue feels, and if only we'd got somewhere else to go, I'd clear out at once, contract or no contract."

"Now listen, Bob." George Cunningham at last succeeded in making himself heard. "I can answer a lot of your questions and I think I'll be able to help you, but first of all I'd like to check that Sue's all right."

"She's fast asleep."

"I know, but I'd like to look at her, please."

Bob gave him a somewhat suspicious glance and then led the way to the bedroom door and stood silent while George bent over the unconscious girl.

"What's the matter?" he asked when George had laid Sue's hand back on the bedspread. "Is there something wrong?"

"She's taken too many sleeping tablets, but she'll be all right."

"Those bloody pills!" shouted Bob, and then he sat down suddenly on the end of the bed and put his face in his hands. George put a hand on his shoulder. It was plain that the boy was not far from a total nervous collapse. Perhaps this was why he had not seemed sufficiently sympathetic to his wife; it was only with great effort that he was keeping going himself. George blamed himself for not realising how much Bob Merry had been suffering from all the troubles at Digby Hall. These young men who seemed so tough and competent. One tended to forget that they could have their troubles too.

Nancy had been quite right to say that pretence must end and they must all help each other. At any rate the four of them, himself and Nancy, Bob and Sue. Together they would fight and stamp out this evil thing that had ruined the tranquility of this lovely old house and garden in which a variety of old and lonely people had found something of the comfort and companionship of a home.

"Take it easy, Bob," said George. "You're going to be all right, and so is Sue. But I'd like you to hold on to her tablets for her. And keep an eye on her. And I'm going to keep an eye on you both. It's going to be all right, Bob. I'll tell you about it if you're feeling better."

The young man's trembling seemed to be abating and he muttered a word of thanks.

"Then let's go back to the sitting room," said George.

He accepted a glass of sherry and they were just about to seat themselves, Bob looking much calmer and more amenable now, when the telephone rang.

"Damn," said Bob. "At this hour."

"Could be Miss Pick phoning for me."

"No. It's the outside line." Bob lifted the receiver. "Yes? Yes?" He spoke impatiently, his face twisting uncontrollably. He really was in a bad state of nerves. "Bloody call box," he muttered, and then, a moment later: "Yes. Mr. Merry speaking."

For the next few seconds he seemed to listen in silence, and George, watching him anxiously, saw his expression change from agitated irritation to something that looked more like fear.

"Who are you? Who's that speaking?" cried Bob at last. "Don't go—don't go! Give me the number and I'll ring back . . . don't go!"

There was hysteria in the rise of the voice. George Cunningham felt a sudden coldness of apprehension. Bob began to swear loudly, dropped the receiver and then grabbed it back again and dialled three times.

"Operator, operator, I've got to trace a call . . . Just come from a call box . . . but I must trace it! I must! . . . What d'you mean, you can't do anything! I've got to know who it was. There must be something you can do."

A moment's silence. Then Bob Merry's voice again, more and more out of control.

"Oh, all right then. If that's all you can do. Go ahead

and intercept all calls coming through to this number . . .
Talk about locking the stable door after the horse has
bolted . . . I'll just have to be satisfied, won't I? I've no
alternative."

He slammed the receiver down and rounded on George.
"And you can clear out right away. I've had enough. I don't
want any explanations. I don't want you here now. Nor at
any time. Get me? We don't want to see you. Nor anybody
else. Sue and I will look after ourselves."

George Cunningham was on his feet, backing towards the
door. There was a wild look in the young man's eye. He
advanced threateningly and then suddenly stopped, turned,
drank the rest of his sherry, picked up George's glass and
drained that too, and then picked up the bottle and refilled
his own.

"Get out, get out!" he shouted.

George Cunningham did so. He really had no choice.
A minute later he was telling Nancy.

"The phone call," she said.

"That's what did it. He was calming down nicely and we
could have cleared things up."

"A call box," she said thoughtfully.

"Yes. Could be anybody."

"Could be Mrs. Langford."

"Or Mrs. Ramsden."

"Or Mr. Jonathan Langford. Now that's a man I don't
trust, the little I've seen of him," said Nancy. "He's been
doing his best to make Sue feel she's at fault."

"But he had nothing to do with Mr. Horder's death."

"I know. Oh George." The brisk and capable Nancy Pick
sounded very near to tears. "If only you and I had had this
talk before, we might have been able to do something."

George Cunningham patted her hand as it lay on the arm
of the brown leather chair. It was a large hand, roughened
and wrinkled, and the nails were not very clean. "I know,"
he said. "That's just what I've been thinking myself. But
after all, we have done something. We've saved Sue's life.
And if we have lost Bob's confidence, at least he is now on
the alert. And he can't turn me out of Digby Hall. And I'll

tell Dr. Mercer about Sue. Oh yes, there'll be plenty of things we can do."

Nancy did not look much comforted. "It's these telephone calls," she said. "There's no way we can stop them. And there's nothing worse when you are in a state of nerves than having a mysterious phone call. The obscene ones are horrible. I used to get them sometimes when I had my bungalow, but the ones where you lift the receiver and nobody speaks are even worse."

"There was certainly speaking in this one to Bob," said George.

"But what can have been said," cried Nancy, "to have such an effect on him?"

They looked at each other in consternation and despair.

8

"Thank you, sister." Amy Langford raised her head slightly from the pillow and smiled her martyr's smile. "I shan't need the telephone any more tonight. I got through to my son's flat."

The night sister unplugged the flex and trundled the movable call box towards the door of the little room. Then she returned to the bed and made a quite unnecessary adjustment to the patient's pillows. She didn't like Mrs. Langford, and she could not explain why, although she had many years of nursing experience and much experience of human nature. One could not exactly say that Mrs. Langford had been a difficult patient. Considering how very ill she had been, and what she had been through, she was by no means excessively demanding. She did what she was told and cooperated with the treatment as far as her condition allowed.

Yet the night sister, and indeed all the other nursing staff, felt that they would be glad when she had gone. It hadn't been so bad when she was in a high fever, and the bruises and minor injuries needed attending to, but when the critical stages were past and the patient had sunk into this state of

extreme weakness and mental confusion, the night sister
had begun to feel this revulsion—yes, it really was
revulsion—towards Mrs. Langford.

"How was your son?" she asked. There was no reason
why she should linger, and she had plenty of things she
ought to be doing, but Mrs. Langsford always gave you the
feeling that you ought to be attending to her, or that you
were not attending to her properly. Nothing was ever said. It
was just a sort of aura that she exuded. She even made you
feel as if you had to put on a special sort of voice to talk to
her, a sort of "handle with care" voice, softer, gentler, and
above all, falser than the one you used with other patients.

Falseness. That was it. Everything about this patient just
reeked of falseness, although all the doctors had sworn that
the weakness and the confusion were not put on, and what
could a nurse do but accept the higher medical judgement?
The night sister was a kind and honest woman, calm and
patient, seldom out of temper. Mrs. Langford induced in her
a most unwonted irritation. The faint whine of the voice
grated on her like chalk on a blackboard.

"He's coming down from London tomorrow," said that
voice, "to arrange for me to go home. To Digby Hall, that
is. I suppose I have to call it home, since I have no other.
And it would have felt like home perhaps, if only my very
dear friend . . ."

The voice trailed away into suppressed sobs. This was the
usual reaction to the slightest reference to the dead Mr.
Horder. Of course if they really had been going to get
married it was quite natural, thought the night sister trying
to fight down her impatience. It really was a most terrible
thing to have happened to the poor woman. But all the
same, the little irreverent thought would keep popping up:
what a life that poor man would have had with her! Perhaps
he was better dead.

Feeling guilty at these thoughts, the night sister then
stayed chatting even longer, much to Mrs. Langford's
annoyance. Amy found these little bright conversations a
very great strain, and there seemed to be more and more of
them as she got better. For the sake of policy she was having

to act the Amy of the old days, Philip's Amy, and she
herself found this old Amy just as irritating as everybody
else did. The pretence of mental confusion was far less
strain, because it had developed so naturally. At first it
really had been all confusion, pain, and the terror and
helplessness of nightmare. There was no question of
pretending, or of anything at all except surviving.

Then it began to sort out a little, and the pain eased, and
she knew she was Amy and remembered some things. Not
much, but something very beautiful and precious. Looking
across at a landscape of green hills and bright blue sky. That
was the memory that had come back to her when she opened
her eyes and recognised Jonathan. The sunny sky and the
hills were linked with a friend and perhaps she would marry
him.

It was a happy thought among all the darkness and
confusion that still overwhelmed her for much of the time.
She tried to hold on to it, but faces and voices kept coming
with their questions, talking of cars running out of control,
and people drowning, demanding that she bring forth other
memories, begging her, pleading with her to remember.

How had she come to the crouching, semiupright with
her legs entangled in the steering wheel, in a car that was
tipped on its side in the mud at the side of the river?

"Trying to get help," she had muttered, and that had
seemed to satisfy them a little. "My head. Oh, my head!"
she went on.

It ached terribly when they asked questions. She remembered it aching terribly in the car. The sun was so hot. She
couldn't escape it. Yet her feet were cold in the water. And
in the water there was a dead man.

They asked more questions.

"He's dead, he's drowned!" she cried and began to sob
and cry so much that the questioning voices went away and
one of the white-coated figures came and told her to
swallow something.

After that it began to sort out in her mind and she could
see it all clearly, as if she was looking at it on a cinema
screen. There was this man standing on the bank of the

river, and there was this woman who was going to run the
car down the slope at him. It was very clever, the way she
did it. Amy was full of admiration as she watched the screen
in her mind. The placing of the stone, the releasing of the
brake, the removal of the stone—how very simple and
effective.

But at that point the picture became blurred. The
woman's actions were no longer clear. It was all muddle and
terror. Amy didn't even know whether she was taking part
in the film or watching it. The whole thing was so
dreamlike. She was doing it and looking on it both at the
same time. When they asked questions Amy began to
answer them as if she were watching the film.

"She's trying to climb out of the car . . . she's trying to
get help."

In the end they stopped asking. That was a relief. It
meant that she could allow herself to think about other
things. Digby Hall and the people there. They were all quite
clear in her mind and she hated them as much as ever. It was
all their fault that her friend was dead, and she would never
know any more of those happy moments. The moment itself
began to stretch out longer and longer, ceased to be a
memory, turned into the start of a glorious future that her
enemies had destroyed for her.

Amy saw it as if on the screen. She and her friend were
walking hand in hand, she could see their backs, hand in
hand over the green hills into the sunset. Sweet music was
playing. It was all light and happiness. And these jealous
spiteful people had destroyed it. There was nothing left for
her now but to take her revenge. Oh, the sweet blessed joy
of planning revenge! That was the healing cup, not all these
pills and potions that they kept bringing her.

It was Jonathan who gave her the idea for striking the first
blow; Jonathan, who had once been so neglectful, now
could not do too much for her. He was up and down from
London nearly every day to visit her, brought flowers that
she barely glanced at, fruit that she could not be bothered to
eat, books and magazines that did not interest her.

At first his visits were rather a strain. It didn't take long to tell him all she knew about her friend Mr. Horder, and how he had been going to look for this very special orchid for her. After that, conversation dragged. Neither of them wanted to remember the past, and Amy had not the least interest in Jonathan's work. She took refuge in her mental confusion, and he consoled himself by criticising the running of Digby Hall.

"They ought to have some older responsible person in charge, not just that girl who's got no qualifications at all."

Amy did not remark that this had not worried Jonathan at the time when he had forced her to go and live at Digby Hall. She was not interested in quarrelling with Jonathan or in making him feel guilty. He no longer mattered to her, except as a means of carrying out her revenge.

"It's scandalous," she agreed. "I don't think the Committee can have the slightest idea of what goes on there, or they would do something about it."

The rest of that visit passed off very comfortably. They had found a topic of conversation that interested them both and held them together. Thus it was that Amy decided her next target should be Sue. It really would be a good idea to get rid of Sue Merry, because Amy had never been quite sure what Mrs. Graham had told her. Obviously it had been nothing very definite, or it would somehow have come out into the open, but it might have been enough to start Sue thinking along undesirable lines.

The line to take with Sue was to keep her feeling very worried and even guilty. Apparently Jonathan, without any prompting from Amy, had already done good work in that direction. With only the slightest of nudges, he could be induced to carry it on. He also acted as a useful informant. There was no need to appear confused with Jonathan. He knew she was doing quite a lot of pretending, but he backed her up against the powers that be, without her having to prompt him at all. Through Jonathan she learnt all about the inquest and what had been said, and the very nervous state that Mrs. Merry was in. She also learnt that the Committee had clammed up together and that even his friend the Chairman was reluctant to hear any criticism of the running of the place.

Of course Jonathan could not tell her what was being said by the young Merrys and the remaining residents of Digby Hall, but Lorna Ramsden filled in those gaps. She visited Amy frequently, and at first Amy had been very muddled and distressed, for she could not tell what Lorna's attitude towards her was going to be, and it seemed safer that way. After all, they had been sort of rivals for the attentions of Mr. Horder, and Lorna would be justified in accusing Amy of carrying him off under her nose.

Lorna made no such accusation. Apparently the excitement of the whole affair far outweighed any little jealousy or resentment. Nevertheless, Amy thought it advisable to play down the romantic side of it.

"People will exaggerate so," she complained. "There was nothing in it—between him and me, I mean. He wanted to show me those flowers—you know how mad he was about botany. I wasn't really all that keen, because you know how exhausting it is being with someone who is so deaf, but I thought it would be a kindness . . . and of course it's always nice to have a little outing."

Lorna seemed to forgive her. Amy did not trust this forgiveness, but it was safest to pretend that she did. And after all, the outing had ended disastrously, which must surely have made Lorna feel more kindly towards Amy. After a while they settled into something approaching their former relationship, although Amy could not feel that she had quite the same degree of dominance that she had had before. It was a great disadvantage to be in a hospital bed, and to be shut away in some convalescent home would be little better. In fact, the only thing was to go back to Digby Hall itself, for there was no other way in which she could carry through her revenge. Sowing the seed in Jonathan's mind was no trouble at all. He seemed to see no inconsistency between his own diatribes against the place on the one hand and his determination that his mother should go back there on the other. Amy listened in silence to his suggestion that she should have a nurse-companion in the adjoining flat. She had not the slightest intention of submitting for long to any such supervision, but until the inquest on Mr. Horder was safely over it was essential that she should show no signs of being able to look after herself.

There was no reason why she should not plan for future action, however, and it was after a visit from Lorna Ramsden that Amy had the idea of the telephone calls.

"The place is like a morgue," Lorna had grumbled, "and mealtimes are worse than ever. You feel you have to apologise if you dare to speak, and as for a bit of laugh— they all glare at you as if you've committed blasphemy."

"Let me try and think now," Amy had said, frowning. "Who is there now at Digby Hall?"

"Dr. Cunningham, who's become so short and bad-tempered, you can't imagine. Even Mrs. Gurney seems to have gone off him. And Nancy Pick, who seems to be in a permanent state of sulks. And young Bob Merry has turned quite rude. I don't think much of these long-haired youngsters, but at least he used to be friendly enough. While, as for his wife—well, if you ask me, that one is heading for a total nervous breakdown, and believe me, I've seen some. I know the symptoms."

"Oh dear," said Amy. "Poor Mrs. Merry. And she used to be such a bright little thing."

With this encouragement, Lorna embarked on details. The cooking had gone off terribly; the house was never cleaned; nobody brought your letters to your apartment; Mrs. Merry burst into tears if you even spoke to her, and if you ever dared to ask for anything or make the least hint of a complaint—well, she just ran away and shut herself in the warden's flat and wouldn't answer the door or the telephone.

Amy listened with interest.

"Do you mean she won't answer outside calls either? Or just the internal lines to the warden's flat?"

"Oh, I suppose she answers outside calls," replied Lorna. "She'd have to, wouldn't she? It might be one of the Committee."

"Or a friend or relative of hers. She's got a mother somewhere, I believe," said Amy. "In Glasgow, I think. Does some sort of job."

She managed to make it sound as if living in Glasgow and doing a sort of job were things that no self-respecting person would admit to, then suddenly remembered that Lorna Ramsden herself was of Scottish origin and had also done some sort of job, if you counted the years she had spent running what Amy was sure had been a very nasty and below par little nursing home.

"Being so far away, I suppose Mrs. Merry wouldn't think to ask her mother to come and help," said Amy with a slight change of tone.

"I don't suppose the Committee would want that," said Lorna. "After all, if you're paying a warden, she's got to do the job, and if she's not fit for it, then she's got to go. Suppose Sue's mother came along and turned out to be another Mrs. Gurney! Can't you imagine the fur flying."

She leant back in her chair and her raucous laugh filled the little room. Amy felt one of her headaches coming on. These, at least, were genuine, and she suffered quite a lot from them. Although she did not complain much, the medical staff could see they were genuine and it helped to keep up the impression of weakness and confusion. Luckily a nurse came in at this moment and, catching the look of pain and desperation in Amy's eye, decreed that the visitor must go.

"Thank you," murmured Amy a minute later when peace had been restored to the room. Lorna was only just tolerable when you were on your feet and had full control over her. But when you were in a helpless position yourself . . . Never mind. Her turn would come, and meanwhile she was being useful.

"I'll bring you some tablets," said the nurse, looking down on the drooping eyelids and the uncontrollable twitching of the features that accompanied these headaches.

"Oh, thank you," said Amy. "And please may I have the telephone call box—if nobody's using it and if you don't mind fetching it."

"Of course. If you're sure you're fit to make a call."

"I'll feel better when I've made it," said Amy.

And she did feel better.

It was wonderful to feel powerful again after all the helplessness of hospital and illness; the having to be sweet and polite to everyone because your comfort depended on them. Oh, it was like a tonic, it was better than all the medicines there were, to have someone quavering at the sound of your voice, even though they did not know it was your voice.

Any telephone call can be a strain for somebody in a very nervous condition, and an even worse one when it comes from a call box. Amy pressed in the coin when she heard the signal, and then waited in silence while the voice at the other end of the wire became more and more agitated.

"Who's there? Who is it? Who are you? Why don't you speak?"

When she judged that the girl was just on the point of dropping the receiver or calling somebody else to the phone, Amy began to speak, very close to the mouthpiece, in a low breathy voice. To her own ears it sounded rather like one of the robot monsters of a children's television programme, and the thought made her want to giggle, but since the absurd whisper seemed to be having an effect on the hearer, she controlled herself and continued with it.

"Why didn't you answer Mrs. Graham's phone when she called you in the night?" said the threatening, panting voice. "She might be alive now if you'd answered her phone."

There was a little scream on the other end of the wire and then the questioning began again, more and more frantic and hysterical. Amy replaced the receiver and leant back against her pillows. When the nurse came to take away the call box, Amy was sleeping peacefully.

She limited the number of calls to the times when she judged Bob Merry would be out at his classes, and on the one occasion when she heard his voice on the line, Amy replaced the receiver without speaking. It was very important not to overdo it. The softening up of the victim was her aim, not the sort of persecution that could lead to having the Post Office intercept all calls, or to some other retaliatory action.

It was very frustrating not to be able to ask Lorna
Ramsden straight out what effect her tactics were having,
but at least she did get a bit of information from Lorna. Sue
Merry was getting worse and worse, and even when the
ordeal of the inquest was over, she showed no signs of
improvement. Lorna had seen her coming out of Dr.
Cunningham's apartment in tears, quite beside herself.
She—Lorna—had made some excuse for calling on Dr.
Cunningham, and had turned the conversation round to the
subject of Mrs. Merry, saying she didn't seem to be fit to do
her job. Dr. Cunningham had replied very snappily that it
was no use nagging at the girl, that she'd be all right if
people would treat her with consideration, and that in his
opinion it wouldn't hurt the remaining residents to get all
their own meals and look after themselves and their
apartments and the public rooms of the house until Mrs.
Merry had recovered enough to attend to her duties again.

"He said he and Miss Pick were prepared to do so,"
continued Lorna to the eagerly listening Amy, "and he
didn't see why I shouldn't do the same. Speak for yourself, I
thought; after all, we're paying through the nose to have a
certain amount of service—heaven knows it's little enough
at the best of times, and with the way things are now—"

Amy managed to get her back from general grievances to
the subject of Sue Merry. Lorna did not have anything much
to add, but at least Amy learnt that there was no question of
the girl's mother being sent for at the moment, and that Bob
Merry was still going the two evenings each week to his
classes and spending a lot of time on his studies that, in
Lorna Ramsden's opinion, ought to be spent on looking
after his wife and after the comfort of the residents of Digby
Hall. After all, he was paid to do so.

"I don't think Bob is actually paid anything," said Amy
sweetly. "He has the use of the flat in return for doing odd
jobs about the place."

Lorna snorted. "He's living off his wife then. It's
disgusting."

"Do you think Sue resents that?" prompted Amy with
very little hope of extracting anything worth hearing. Using

Lorna Ramsden as a tool for dissecting the most subtle and intimate human relations was rather like trying to take a wristwatch to pieces with a pair of pliers. Mixed with her increasing impatience and despair, Amy became conscious of another sensation: that of great loneliness. It was nothing to do with feeling neglected or not having anybody to talk to. It went much deeper than that and was very painful, a great yawning ache that seemed to blacken and envelop all her world.

Nothing could ease it, not even the very clever scheme that was forming in her mind, and the delight in her own power. It was a great burden of pain and it had been with her always, all her life, only she had never known it until now.

A friend. Why had she never had a friend who would see things as she did, who would know how to use the tweezers instead of the pliers? Somebody who would understand straightaway, without needing all the little things explained; somebody to share the scheming with. But there had never been such a friend. They had all been so stupid. So stupid. Like Lorna.

Why had nobody ever told Amy she needed a friend to share her mind with? Why had nobody ever told Amy she wasn't stupid?

"Good evening, Mrs. Langford," said the night sister as she came into the room. "Everything all right?"

"Yes, thank you," said the mask of the woman who had always had a mind but never a friend.

"Do you want the call box?"

"Later on, if you will be so kind. It's no use ringing my son until after nine."

The nurse left the room. Amy returned to her terrible emptiness. She ought to be making her call to Sue Merry. Bob would be out, and the girl alone in the warden's flat. But she could not do it. It no longer seemed to matter. Her own emptiness and despair were too great. She did not know that the call would have been unnecessary, that Sue Merry had already been given away to her own despair.

Amy lay with her emptiness for another hour before she summoned up the will to make the call. By that time Sue

had been rescued and Dr. Cunningham was trying to calm
the nerves of Sue's husband. When Amy had pressed in the
coin and heard Bob's voice, her first instinct had been to put
the phone down without speaking. It was the lonely
emptiness that drove her on. If she didn't speak now she
was going to feel even worse than she had felt before.

She made her voice very low, a breathless whisper, not
the measured panting voice in which she spoke to Sue.

"Don't trust anybody." These were the first words that
came into her mind. "There's enemies all round you. Very
near to you. They are after your wife. Don't trust anybody.
Anybody at all."

That was all she could manage and it exhausted her. The
young man's frantic questioning gave her no pleasure.
There was no satisfaction in picturing the scene of bewilderment and fear, no savour of triumph. The emptiness was
still there. Perhaps I am after all very ill, thought Amy. It
comforted only for a moment. Medical attention she had in
plenty and it didn't even begin to touch her grief.

Trying not to think at all, she raised herself up again from
the pillows and found another coin. Jonathan answered the
phone quickly. She got him to ring back on his own line,
and then she summoned up her last remaining strength to
tell him how very much better she was feeling and how she
was longing to get out of hospital and back to normal life.

Jonathan had been making enquiries about a suitable
person to take up residence in Digby Hall as a nurse-
companion to his mother, but nothing definite had yet been
fixed. It was the Digby Hall end that was causing the
holdup. He had several very suitable candidates, but
apparently the Committee had not taken very kindly to the
idea. Even his friend the Chairman was proving unexpect-
edly obstinate.

Amy felt a great lurch of despair, tried to speak, but
failed.

"Hullo? Are you still there, Mother?" cried Jonathan.

"Yes, dear." It was all she could manage, but it sounded
all right.

"I was wondering whether you might not like to go to a
convalescent home for a while. Just while I am sorting out

the difficulties about your going back to Digby Hall. They'll have to give in in the end, but it may take longer than I thought, and this would at least get you out of hospital.''

A strange convalescent home. Whatever use was that to Amy? No, there was only one place where her emptiness might be eased, and that was Digby Hall. Not among her friends, for she had none, but among her enemies. All of them there were her enemies. It filled the blankness, to have enemies.

"Are you listening, Mother? Are you all right?"

Jonathan sounded more impatient than anxious. Terror that she might lose her ascendancy over him sharpened Amy's wits.

"Yes, dear," she replied in a stronger voice. "I don't know what to say. I'd hoped so much to go straight back to Digby Hall. You see, it's got memories for me."

Jonathan was sympathetic. He could quite understand how his mother felt. After all, it was at Digby Hall that she had met Mr. Horder. Of course she would have memories. In fact, Amy had temporarily quite forgotten Mr. Horder and was grateful to Jonathan for reminding her of this, her strongest weapon.

"I'm so glad you understand, dear," she said. "I really don't want to be anywhere else."

Jonathan promised to have another go at the Digby Hall authorities. The following afternoon he visited Amy in person to announce his success. She was to go back to her old flat at the end of the week. The apartment next door would be put at the disposal of Mrs. Mary Fairfax, a retired doctor's receptionist, who took on temporary light nursing jobs from time to time and who fortunately happened to be free.

"Mrs. Fairfax," repeated Amy.

She was dressed and seated at the side of the bed. Her face was turned away from Jonathan and he could not judge her reaction at all.

"She has excellent references," he said.

"Oh. References?" Amy turned to look at him. Her expression was quite blank.

"References," repeated Jonathan irritably. "As if I should put you into the care of anybody without taking up their references."

He was annoyed by her total lack of response after all the trouble he had gone to, but at the same time relieved that she showed no curiosity about Mrs. Fairfax, who was in fact not one of the suitable middle-aged widows on Jonathan's short list, but had only cropped up that very morning, when Jonathan had gone to Digby Hall to keep an appointment made with Mr. Ernest Fisher.

In the face of trouble, Mr. Fisher was turning out to be the strongest force in the adminstration of Digby Hall. He also provided the strongest opposition to Jonathan's plan of bringing his mother back there. Late the previous night, Mr. Fisher had come round to Digby Hall at Dr. Cunningham's urgent request, and they had had a very long talk. As a result of that talk, Mr. Fisher had modified his decision, and Jonathan Langford was presented with an ultimatum, right there in the dining room at Digby Hall. They would take his mother back, but they must choose the woman to look after her.

Jonathan was used to issuing ultimatums, not receiving them, and he did not like Mr. Fisher's manner. Neither did Mr. Fisher like Jonathan's. The previous evening he had told George Cunningham that all the troubles at Digby Hall stemmed from the fact that the Committee had allowed Jonathan Langford to bulldoze his mother past the waiting list, and Dr. Cunningham had whole-heartedly agreed.

Mr. Fisher set out the qualifications of Mrs. Fairfax and actually produced copies of her references. One of them was for George Cunningham himself. She had worked for him for some years when he was in general practice. The others were impeccable as well. She was willing to do the job for a very modest salary, and Digby Hall would not charge Jonathan anything for her accommodation.

Jonathan Langford was being offered a solution to his problem at very little cost and at no trouble to himself, yet such was his dislike of the man sitting opposite him across

the dining-room table that he could only just bring himself
to accept it.

"Supposing my mother does not take to Mrs. Fairfax?"
he said.

"You are at liberty to seek other accommodation for
her," said Mr. Fisher.

"I resent being hustled like this," said Jonathan.

"No doubt you will require some time to think over the
suggestion. That is quite reasonable," said Mr. Fisher.

They stared at each other, the little dried-up elderly man,
and the rather overweight, rather florid younger man. If I
don't accept, thought Jonathan, she's going to be forever
pestering me, and I'll still have to find somewhere for her to
live. If he refuses, thought Mr. Fisher, then it's no longer
our worry, but it will leave us with a very uneasy conscience
because, if there is anything in this fantastic idea of George
Cunningham's, then we shall be unleashing a dangerous
woman upon some other unsuspecting and innocent little
community.

There was a silence. Jonathan knew he was going to
accept, because he really had no tolerable alternative. Mr.
Fisher knew that in his heart he wanted Jonathan to accept,
whatever the outcome might be, because he was by nature a
fighter and he did not like running away from a challenge.

"Am I permitted to inspect this—er—Mrs. Fairfax?"
said Jonathan at last.

"She's waiting in the foyer," said Mr. Fisher.

9

Once again there were eight places set on the dark mahogany table in the dining room. But some of the flagstones on the terrace were in shadow, even in the middle of the day, and the brown beech leaves were piling up at the edges of the lawn. It was three months since Clement Horder had died, and since then there had been no more deaths at Digby Hall.

The six people now seated at the table all looked in good health, though Sue Merry was still rather pale and subdued. She had made a chicken casserole and the big oven dish, still steaming, was on the table in front of her. Bob, sitting next to her, was about to help her serve, but stopped at a word and a gesture from Mr. Ernest Fisher, who was sitting at the far end of the table.

"Shall we wait for the others?" said Mr. Fisher. "I think it would be only courteous, as it is Mrs. Langford's first day down since she came back to Digby Hall."

The Merrys murmured agreement.

"I don't suppose they'll be long," said Nancy Pick, glancing at George Cunningham who was sitting next to her, with Sue Merry at the end of the table on his other side.

He looked a little apprehensive, Nancy thought. In fact,
they were all rather apprehensive, except perhaps Mrs.
Ramsden, who was not in the plot, and who was now
looking very irritable at having to wait for her meal. Mr.
Fisher looked just the same as he always did. It had been a
great comfort to George when Mr. Fisher said he would
move into Mr. Horder's flat in order to be on the premises.
Nancy had been relieved too. It was almost like having a
resident detective. Better, in fact, because no detective,
however brilliant, could possibly know the ways of Digby
Hall and the personalities involved as well as Mr. Fisher
did.

Nancy felt a lot safer with Mr. Fisher there, but she still
did not feel completely at ease, because that was too much
to expect when you were living under the same roof as a
woman who might well be a murderer. True, she had a
"keeper" in the form of a nurse-companion, and Nancy did
not envy Mrs. Fairfax her job, but such a devilishly
ingenious mind could surely outwit even the keenest
observer. And after all, it was no use hoping that nothing
would happen, because then there would never be any
proof.

The fact that she, and George, and Mr. Fisher, and the
Merry's were now all convinced that Mrs. Langford had
brought about the deaths of two human beings and had
aimed to drive Sue Merry to suicide, did not constitute
proof. The only thing approaching hard evidence was Sue's
assertion that the voice on the telephone could have been
Mrs. Langford's. She had admitted this to George and Mr.
Fisher, when their combined efforts had at last broken down
the resistence of the young couple. George had chatted to
the hospital sister and learnt that Mrs. Langford had
frequently asked for the movable call box in the evening.

It's a great pity, thought Nancy, that it always keeps
coming back to poor little Sue. It was very brave of her to
insist on staying on at Digby Hall after Mr. Fisher had
explained the plan.

"I'm certainly not going to kill myself," Sue had said,

"and if she tries to get at me in any other ways—well, I've got Bob. We'll protect each other."

At least that was one thing gained. Sue and Bob had been very close since the big explanation scene. Yet there were bound to be times when she was at risk, not to mention the possibility of a long-distance operation. Poisoning, for example.

Nancy's eyes moved to the big oven dish. Its contents smelt very good. But suppose those mushrooms happened to be poisonous toadstools? Suppose the jar out of which the salt had been taken contained not only harmless household salt but some other substance? It was no use telling oneself that Mrs. Langford had no opportunity to get at the kitchen store-cupboard, let alone get hold of any poison. These were the sort of speculations that were bound to arise in the circumstances. And it was no use telling oneself that the whole thing was too absurd and melodramatic to be true. The telephone calls that had driven Sue Merry to desperation were very real. Mrs. Graham's death was true enough, and so was Mr. Horder's.

On the other hand, everybody agreed that Mrs. Graham's death had every appearance of being a natural one; and noboby could deny that Mrs. Langford herself had suffered severely in the accident that led to Mr. Horder's death. Supposing Mrs. Langford had in fact been responsible, but that her fit of homicidal mania was now over, and her memory of events before the accident had gone forever. In that case there was no hope of her giving herself away about the past, and no hope, if one could indeed "hope" for such a thing, of her attempting another murder in the future. No proof would ever be forthcoming; no progress would ever be made. They would go on indefinitely as they were at present—keeping watch over a confused, but now harmless, elderly woman.

It was a depressing thought, even more depressing than the prospect of fresh disasters. Nancy was quite glad when Mrs. Ramsden's voice broke into her speculations.

"Would you mind passing me the water jug? Or do I have to wait for that too?"

Nancy reached for the jug. "I'm sure they won't be long now," she murmured soothingly.

"Ridiculous," said Mrs. Ramsden without troubling to lower her voice. "Nobody ever used to wait for me when I was late for a meal."

"But Mrs. Langford has been very ill," said Nancy.

"And who's fault was it in the first place? Dragging that poor man out like that when he wasn't fit to be driving."

"But Mr. Horder was quite competent to drive," said Nancy.

"That's what *you* think," retorted Mrs. Ramsden darkly.

Nancy caught Mr. Fisher's eye and saw him frown very slightly. She interpreted this to mean that Mrs. Ramsden should not be encouraged to talk like that at this moment. It was a pity, because it looked as if it might lead to something, and Nancy rather fancied doing a little detective work on her own. However, the door of the room was being pushed open wide, and Mrs. Fairfax's voice, gentle but authoritative, was to be heard.

"Look, they're waiting for us. That's a nice welcome, isn't it?"

The woman who was clinging to her arm did not speak. She looked rather thinner then she had in the early summer, but the face still had its pink doll-like look, and the grey hair was clean and neat. Nancy Pick thought the floral-patterned afternoon frock was too dressy for the occasion, but then she always did think that Mrs. Langford looked over-dressed. One couldn't say, though, that she looked either like a raving lunatic or like a very sick woman neglecting her appearance. She just looked a bit lost, which was hardly surprising in the circumstances. In fact, Mrs. Fairfax, who had spent a lot of time with her in her apartment since her return to Digby Hall, had reported that she really did seem to be suffering from loss of memory.

Nancy felt more and more depressed as the two women approached the table and sat down, Mrs. Langford next to Mr. Fisher, and Mrs. Fairfax between Mrs. Langford and Bob Merry. This is a mistake, thought Nancy as, after a few halfhearted murmurs of welcome, silence fell on the table.

Sue and Bob made a great deal of work out of serving and handing round the meal; Mrs. Fairfax glanced anxiously at her patient; Dr. Cunningham and Mr. Fisher frowned and looked at nothing; and Mrs. Langford herself sat there like a zombie.

This is frightful, thought Nancy; we simply cannot go on like this. But she could think of nothing to say. Once again it was Mrs. Ramsden who came to the rescue.

"Very nice," she said after taking a few mouthfuls from her plate. "Is this to celebrate the prodigal's return?"

Nancy felt so grateful that she was even able to forgive Mrs. Ramsden her laugh. Everybody praised the cooking, and the awkwardness began to ease. Remarks were made about the weather and the garden and last night's television play that several of them had watched. Only Mrs. Langford remained completely silent, eating steadily and not looking around at all. At one point, Mrs. Ramsden leant across the table and said loudly, "Feeling better now, Amy?" as if she was addressing a deaf person.

Mrs. Langford took no notice at all.

"Whatever's the matter with her?" asked Mrs. Ramsden addressing the table at large. "She's worse than she was in hospital!"

There was a moment's silence in which everybody looked uneasy except Mrs. Langford herself. Then Mrs. Fairfax spoke.

"It's rather a strain, being among people again after one has been ill for some time."

Several people, led by George Cunningham, hastily began to relate personal experiences that bore out this statement. Nancy Pick did not join them. We can't possibly go on like this, she was saying to herself; not with all this strain and falseness.

Sue Merry removed the plates and handed round the individual dishes of peach melba. At last the nightmarish meal drew to an end. Mrs. Fairfax put down her spoon and pushed back her chair. "If you'll excuse us," she said, "I think this is enough for a first time." She touched Mrs. Langford's arm. "Are you ready to go?"

Mrs. Langford dabbed at her mouth with her table napkin, folded it neatly and laid it on the polished wood, and then sat with her fingers resting lightly on the edge of the table. She looked like a good little girl at a party, awaiting a signal to move.

"I think we had better have our coffee upstairs," said Mrs. Fairfax.

Mrs. Langford got to her feet. her fingers were still pressed lightly against the edge of the table. She looked around, her eyes resting for a moment on each one of those present in turn. Then at last she spoke.

"Where is Mr. Horder? I don't see Mr. Horder."

It was a small expressionless voice, and the face looked as blank as before. The effect was uncanny. Even Mrs. Ramsden was silenced. Mrs. Fairfax took Mrs. Langford by the arm and tried to lead her away from the table, but the latter shook her off with some violence. It was as if a puppet was beginning to come to life and nobody knew what form the life was going to take.

"Where is he? What have you done with him?"

The voice was rising into fury. The head turned from side to side, all the features twisting in quick convulsive movements. The arms jerked up and the hands came together in a wringing movement.

"Where is he? You've killed him! He was my friend and you've killed him! Aaaaah!"

It was a loud wail, like that of a child, shocking to hear from the mouth of an adult woman. Mrs. Fairfax took her by the arm again and this time had more success. Sobbing and shuddering, and still crying, "You've killed him," Mrs. Langford was induced to leave the room.

"My God," said Dr. Cunningham, taking out a handkerchief and mopping his face.

"Do you think Mrs. Fairfax will be able to manage?" asked Mr. Fisher. Even his equanimity was shaken. Bob and Sue Merry were clinging together; Mrs. Ramsden's florid face had gone quite white, and Nancy felt as if she was going to be sick.

"I'd like to go and help," said George Cunningham,

"but I think I might do more harm than good. If Mrs. Fairfax can't manage, we'll have to phone Dr. Mercer."

"Could I do anything, do you think?" asked Nancy, not wanting to at all but feeling she ought to offer.

George shook his head. "I think we'd better all keep out of it."

"So do I," said Mr. Fisher, getting to his feet. "I am very sorry indeed about this unfortunate occurrence, and I think the kindest thing to be done for Mrs. Langford is for us all to refrain from talking about it."

"Speak for yourself," said Mrs. Ramsden, recovering her colour and her voice. "You may like to hush things up, Mr. Fisher, but Amy Langford's a friend of mine, and if she's gone off her rocker, then I'm certainly going to talk about it. I'm going up to see her now. I've had plenty of experience with this sort of thing, which is more than that Fairfax woman has. It's no good trying to humour them when they get like this. You have to show them who's boss straightaway."

She made such a fine melodramatic exit that Nancy gave a little nervous laugh before she could stop herself. Mr. Fisher looked reproachful. Sue looked more alarmed than ever. "Do you think we ought to warn Mrs. Ramsden?" she whispered.

"No, I don't," said Bob firmly. "Let fools rush in. Let them fight it out together. Anyway, Mrs. Fairfax is up there too."

"Mrs. Fairfax looks to me as if she has had about enough," said George Cunningham in a worried voice.

"And so have I had enough!" Nancy Pick surprised herself by her own vehemence. She had not meant to speak at all, but suddenly it all poured out. "It's impossible to go on like this. Can't you see? Mrs. Langford isn't going to confess to anything. She's going to get more and more suspicious because she knows we're all against her. Look at what happened just now. Accusing us of murdering Mr. Horder! She's turning paranoid and it's not surprising. Anyone would develop persecution mania in the circumstances. I would myself. It's not fair to her. Oh yes, I believe it, all right," she hurried on as George seemed about to interrupt. "I believe it more and more. I think Amy Langford somehow talked Mrs. Graham into moving into the flat next door to her, and that she then got in somehow and persuaded her to leave the door open, or even got round the balcony, and smothered her in a way that left no sign. And I believe she then got friendly with Mr. Horder and persuaded him to take her out and somehow drove his car into the river. Very clever that, managing to escape herself, but maybe it was something to do with his deafness. She's good at working on people's weaknesses, trying to get Sue to kill herself. That's no guesswork. We know it's true. And I'm sure she'll have a go at somebody else because she really is mad in a way, Mrs. Ramden's right about that, but we can't just sit here and wait for it. It isn't fair. It isn't fair to us and it isn't fair to her."

Nancy stopped at last, quite out of breath.

"And what else do you suggest?" said George Cunningham gently.

"I think somebody ought to confront her with it," replied Nancy more calmly. "Tell her straight out what we're suspecting, what I've just been saying, and give her a chance to defend herself."

"Dr. Cunningham and I did discuss such a possibility," said Mr. Fisher, "but we decided that it would be a useless exercise. Mrs. Langford would either deny everything or would break down into a state of such distress that further talk was impossible. This recent outburst would seem to bear that out. And according to Mrs. Fairfax, she barely speaks at all. Mrs. Fairfax has been talking to her a lot about Mrs. Graham and Mr. Horder, not accusing her, but just talking about them, and has met with no response whatever."

"It's the wrong way to set about it!" cried Nancy, thumping her fist upon the back of her chair and becoming very worked up again. "It's no use, this kid-glove business. Anything slinky and subtle and she'll win all along the line. We need shock tactics. Mrs. Ramsden's right about that."

"I wonder how she's getting on," said Bob. "I'd like to

be a fly on the wall." He smiled at Sue, but she did not
smile back.

"I still think we ought to have warned her," she said.
"And I think Miss Pick is right. I think we ought to confront
Mrs. Langford straight out. And I don't mind"—she gasped
and gulped and hurriedly went on—"I don't mind doing it
myself. I'll tell her I recognised her voice on the phone and
I'll even tell her"—she gasped again—"that Mrs. Graham
told me she'd been threatening her if she didn't ask to move
her flat. It's almost true. I mean I knew she'd frightened
Mrs. Graham in some way that made Mrs. Graham ask to
be moved upstairs next to Mrs. Langford. I'll make her
think Mrs. Graham confided in me. And Mr. Horder too.
He was very anxious about that excursion. I'll make her
think he confided in me too. I can do it!" Sue's voice
strengthened into a sort of desperate determination. "I'm
much the best person to do it."

"There's something in that," began Mr. Fisher, "but I
really don't think—"

"Good girl," interrupted Nancy, clapping her hands
together softly. "Well done, Sue. I'll come with you. We'll
do it together."

"She will do nothing of the sort!" shouted Bob, putting
an arm round Sue. "She's had quite enough, thank you. If
anyone's going to stick their necks out, it ought to be Mr.
Fisher and Dr. Cunningham, who insisted on bringing Mrs.
Langford back to Digby Hall."

"I am perfectly prepared to confront Mrs. Langford,"
said George Cunningham with dignity. "I will go and talk to
her at once."

"But George—" Nancy suddenly looked very unhappy.

"You are quite right about the situation being intolerable," he said. "We can't possibly have a repetition of this
mealtime. I'll go up and see what's happening now." He
moved towards the door.

The others looked uneasily at him and then at each other.
They were a divided group, five puzzled and anxious
people. All community of purpose had vanished, and even
Mr. Fisher seemed to have lost his confidence.

But George Cunningham got no further than the door. As he pulled it open, Mrs. Fairfax rushed in, quite unlike her usual composed self.

"I'm giving up!" she cried. "The job's impossible. I don't mind looking after difficult patients, and I don't mind taking a risk when it's a matter of trying to see justice done, and I'd do a lot for you, Dr. Cunningham, because you've been very good to me, but really, really—"

The collapse of Mrs. Fairfax was somehow even more disturbing than Mrs. Langford's outburst had been, but after a cup of coffee and some reassuring words from Dr. Cunningham she recovered and apologised.

"I know I am not supposed to be leaving the patient," she said, "until after I have given her the sleeping drug for the night, but really I could not help it. They pushed me out of the room. Literally. And the language. You've never heard anything like Mrs. Ramsden's language."

Bob Merry gave a little snort and then put his hand to his mouth.

"We know Mrs. Ramsden's language," said Dr. Cunningham. "Go on."

"Well, there isn't really very much more to tell. Mrs. Langford was very distressed after we left the table, and I suggested she should have a lie-down and a cup of tea, and I'd just made it and she seemed to be calming down nicely, thanking me and saying she didn't think she'd come out of her apartment again today and she didn't really feel fit to be with people yet, and we were more or less back to where we had been before, when there came this loud knock on the door, and I said, 'I'll tell them to go away, shall I, dear?' and she said, 'Yes, please, thank you, Mrs. Fairfax,' in a very faint voice. So I opened the door and Mrs. Ramsden pushed in, positively pushed, and I couldn't stop her, and she walked straight over to the divan bed and plumped down on the end of it and said very loudly: 'Now, then, Amy, what are you playing at this time? You've gone and put the cat among the pigeons! You ought to have seen their faces!' And she laughed and laughed—she really has got the most terrbile laugh, hasn't she?"

"What did Mrs. Langford say?" asked Nancy.

They were gathered around Mrs. Fairfax, all five of them, in a little group near the big window that opened onto the terrace. Some were standing, some sitting on the chairs that they had pulled round from the dining table. Sue Merry was replenishing cups of coffee.

"Mrs. Langford didn't do anything at first," said Mrs. Fairfax. "Just lay and stared in that zombie-like way she has. Then Mrs. Ramsden leant forward and patted her hand—though really it was more like a slap—and said, 'Come off it, Amy. You don't need to put on this act with me. Come on. Tell Lorna what it's all about. I've got plenty to tell you if you want to listen. Been dying to come and see you, but that dragon of yours wouldn't let me in.' And she glared at me. Mrs. Ramsden positively glared at me. So I said, 'Excuse me, Mrs. Ramsden, but I am employed to take care of Mrs. Langford, and my orders are that she is not to be disturbed or to talk to anybody if she doesn't want to.' That started up some of the language which I will not repeat, and it ended with her saying in a sort of whining way, very disagreeable, 'But you do want to see me, don't you, Amy dear?' Really I think I almost preferred the swearing, but it did get Mrs. Langford moving, I must say. She got up off the bed and became quite lively, and said: 'Of course I want to see you, Lorna—I've got a fresh bottle of vodka especially for you. Come on. I'm dying for a drink after all these nice cups of tea.' 'But we can't talk with her here,' says Mrs. Ramsden, looking at me. 'Oh, we'll soon get rid of her,' cries Mrs. Langford, and all of a sudden she starts to scream. 'Go away! Leave me alone! I'm sick of being spied on—go away!' I started to say, 'But it's my orders,' and then they both came at me, together, screaming and pushing at me. Well, what can I do?" concluded Mrs. Fairfax, accepting another cup of coffee and one of Sue Merry's homemade shortcakes, "I couldn't fight them both."

"You couldn't possibly do any more," said Dr. Cunningham. "We're very grateful to you for what you've done."

Mr. Fisher added his thanks and said that if Mrs. Fairfax

liked to pack up and go home straightaway, then they would
make up her salary to the end of the month. Mrs. Fairfax
said that was generous, but she didn't think she felt fit to
pack up her things just yet. It was very upsetting, what she
had just been through. There was a moment's silence while
everybody wondered what to do about Mrs. Fairfax's upset,
and then Sue solved the problem by suggesting that Mrs.
Fairfax might like to help her with the washing up, and she
would look up the recipe for the shortcake. They departed,
chatting amicably. Bob said he had some work to prepare
for his tutor when he saw him that evening, and disappeared
up to the warden's flat. Ernest Fisher said he felt like a little
fresh air, and opened the long window that led onto the sun
terrace. George Cunningham and Nancy Pick followed him
out.

There was quite a lot of warmth in the sun. The grass was
shining green after the previous night's rain. A few clusters
of golden leaves still clung to the trees bordering the lawn,
and in the flower beds was the scattered crimson of late
roses. The air was still. Birdsong and the distant hum of
traffic were the only sounds to be heard. Digby Hall seemed
to be bathed in afternoon peace. It was very hard to believe
in malice and murder nearby.

They strolled along the terrace and a little way down the
gravel path.

"Oh, I do love this place!" burst out Nancy suddenly. "I
used to be so happy here."

Her voice shook and she bit her lip. Nancy Pick was
nearer to tears than she had been for a very long time
indeed. The two men glanced at each other. Then George
took her arm.

"And you're going to be happy again," he said. "This
can't go on forever."

"How is it to be stopped? It'll never be the same again."

"It's going to be stopped. It's got to be stopped. I told you
I was going to do something about it."

"I wish you wouldn't, George. Oh yes, I know what I
said just now," went on Nancy quickly. "I do believe that
somebody has got to bring it all out into the open, but I wish
it didn't have to be you."

Mr. Fisher was walking a few yards ahead, just coming up to the kitchen garden. He glanced round for a moment and then hastily looked away and examined some raspberry bushes with great interest. Mr. Fisher was very much a bachelor, but he was by no means without sentiment. In fact, he probably looked upon the elderly lovers with a more kindly eye than many a younger person would have done. Even Bob and Sue, fond of old people though they were, might have found something absurd in the sight of the plump red-faced old man and the scrawny-looking old woman gazing at each other with such tenderness. Mr. Fisher simply said to himself that Mrs. Gurney had better give up her hopes of acquiring Dr. Cunningham as a husband, and made a resolution that if anybody was going to tackle Mrs. Langford straight out, it must be himself.

When the others caught up with him he made a few remarks about the garden and then announced he was going in to think things over.

"Please don't take any action until I have spoken to you again," he added. "Why don't you stay out for a while? We are not likely to get many such afternoons at this time of year."

After he had gone, George Cunningham said: "I believe he's going to do something straightaway."

"I shouldn't be surprised," said Nancy, "and after all, if anyone is going to stick their neck out, it ought to be Mr. Fisher."

They walked on past the cabbage patch.

"Oh look, there's our robin," said Nancy.

"Would you like to go on living here? Or would you rather have your own home?" asked George.

"I'm a rotten housekeeper, and it seems silly to take on the burden of a house at our age."

"I hoped you'd say that," said George, "because I feel the same."

They were at the very bottom of the garden, out of sight of the house. Nancy suddenly began to laugh. "Look here, what are we talking about?"

"What we're going to do when we get married. At least, that's what I thought we were talking about."

"So did I, and then I suddenly wasn't so sure. Are we quite crazy, George? Is it going to ruin everything? We've been such good friends. It would be terrible to spoil it."

George Cunningham tried to explain why he believed their getting married would not spoil it. Nancy Pick gradually allowed herself to be persuaded. They propped themselves against the fence and stared at the cabbages as they talked. For the time being they had completely forgotten about Mrs. Langford and the problems of Digby Hall. The air was crisp with the promise of winter but there was warmth in the sun. They had no need of springtime. They looked without fear and without regrets at the shortening days ahead and at the coming of the cold. There was so much to talk about, so much to look forward to, but there was no need to snatch at it impatiently. They were calmly and deeply happy with the contentment of old age that can live in the present and paradoxically feel a great spaciousness of time just when it's own time is beginning to run out.

—10—

While George and Nancy were experiencing their autumnal idyll at the far end of the kitchen garden, Sue Merry and Mrs. Fairfax were chatting comfortably in the kitchen. They had moved on from recipes to Mrs. Fairfax's experiences as a doctor's receptionist and as a nursing auxiliary. Sue had always wanted to train as a nurse, and they found a lot to talk about. Next door to the kitchen, in the ground-floor flat that had been occupied by Mr. Horder, Mr. Ernest Fisher lit a small cigar, poured himself a small whisky, and sat down to think.

In the warden's flat on the floor above, Bob Merry sat down at the table by the window that was piled high with his books and papers, and tried to apply himself to the theory of supply and demand in classical economics. He was always happier with practical work than with theoretical and he found it hard to concentrate. That scene at lunchtime had been rather upsetting. Perhaps after all it would be best if he and Sue were to leave Digby Hall. On the other hand, she was very much better since the whole business had been brought out into the open, and so was he. Once he had qualified himself with a technology degree, he knew he would be able to get a good job, and they'd never find a more convenient way to live in the meantime than they had at Digby Hall.

Why should they let that vicious old bitch drive them away? If there was going to be trouble, surely he and Sue could keep out of it. It wasn't their responsibility. Mr. Fisher and Dr. Cunningham would have to cope.

After a while Bob managed to calm himself down and get on with his reading. At one point he looked up across the table and out of the window and sniffed. Something burning? Ought he to go down and see if Sue had left a gas jet on? But it didn't smell like cooking. More like wood. A bonfire. They'd be burning the leaves and the garden rubbish at the big house next door. They always did at this time of year. In fact, it was time he did the same at Digby Hall. He'd have a bonfire tomorrow morning if the weather was suitable.

With his mind half on bonfires and half on the diagram at which he was staring, Bob let the impression of the burning smell slip from his consciousness, but it remained somewhere on the margin of awareness, vaguely troubling him, but not disturbing enough to make him get up from his chair.

At the other side of the house, in Amy Langford's apartment, the flames licked across the carpet and caught the curtain that hung over the door to keep out draughts. Mrs. Ramsden, sitting with her back to the door, and facing the long window that opened out onto the balcony, took another big gulp from her glass. They had been talking and drinking ever since Mrs. Fairfax had been pushed out of the room. They had also laughed a great deal. Amy was a scream, taking off all the people in Digby Hall in turn.

"They really think I'm balmy!" she cried. "Did you see their faces when I put on that act just now?"

She was moving about as she talked, but Lorna liked to sit still to drink. The room was becoming rather hazy. And stuffy. And although Amy was obviously perfectly sane, she was nevertheless doing some rather odd things. Picking up newspapers and dropping them on the carpet. Most untidy.

And letting her cigarette ash fall all over the place. That was not only untidy: it was downright foolhardy.

Suddenly Lorna Ramsden's mind cleared and she dropped her glass and staggered to her feet and caught Amy by the arm. For a moment they clung together, staring at the flaming curtain that blocked the door, at the smouldering carpet and cushions, the wallpaper, the bookcase.

Lorna Ramsden gave a stifled scream and looked towards the door that led to the kitchen and bathroom. It was slightly ajar, but flames from the scattered newspapers were leaping towards it.

"Water!" gasped Lorna.

"Too late!" cried Amy. "The balcony. It's our only chance."

"But we can't jump. It's too high."

Lorna Ramsden was giddy and confused again. There was something that puzzled her about this sudden fire, something that her fuddled mind tried to grasp but could not. She wanted to ask Amy some questions, but there was no time to be lost. The flames were gaining everywhere; the smoke was beginning to make breathing difficult.

Amy pushed her towards the balcony.

"You don't need to jump." The voice was low in Lorna's ear. Calm, sweet, and insinuating. Lorna didn't trust the voice, but at least it seemed to be uttering words that made sense. "Get on the balcony, step over the railing to the balcony next door, break the window if it's locked, climb in, and let yourself out of the flat. I'll follow you. All right?"

"All right," muttered Lorna. And it did seem to be all right. Why ever hadn't she thought of it herself? Of course one could get into the neighbouring apartment from the balcony, and once there, escape from the burning room and what was probably going to be the burning house.

Amy pulled open the long window and gave Lorna a little shove to hurry her up.

Lorna Ramsden felt it in the small of her back, and at the same time she tripped over the metal at the bottom of the window frame, tilted forward, and grasped at the flimsy

railing of the balcony to save herself. It was a second or two
before the railing gave way and she fell, headfirst, onto the
hard gravel below. Those seconds of falling seemed like an
eternity in which everything that had been puzzling was
made brilliantly clear.

The balcony. You could get into Mrs. Graham's flat via
the balcony. You could pay a visit to the helpless old woman
and leave the window catch unlocked without her noticing.
You could come in later and smother her, and then get out
through the door. No one would ever know. And Mr.
Horder. That must have been a push. A playful push, but
sharp enough. And the fire. Amy had started the fire herself.

All of this was sharp as lightning in Mrs. Ramsden's
mind before the universe exploded and went black forever.

She was a heavy woman, and George and Nancy heard
the crash as they made their way back from the kitchen
garden towards the house. They ran in the direction of the
sound, and as they ran they saw and smelt the smoke. Bob
Merry, on the first-floor landing, was by this time struggling
with the flames that had made their way through the door of
the apartment. Mr. Fisher was ringing the fire brigade. Only
Sue Merry and Mrs. Fairfax, still in the kitchen, which was
as far as possible from the scene of action, were unaware of
what was happening.

"I can't hold it!" gasped Bob to Ernest Fisher. "And
we'll never get them out this way."

"The window. A ladder."

"O.K."

They ran out of the house and round to the garden shed to
fetch a ladder. They arrived at the side of the house at the
same moment as George and Nancy, coming from the other
direction. On the gravel path, about midway between them,
sprawled Mrs. Ramsden in her emerald-green jersey dress.

"Good God!"

George Cunningham and Bob Merry exclaimed together
and ran forward, one from one side, one from the other.
Neither of them thought to look up, but Nancy did, and that
was how she probably saved George's life. The heavy
pottery jug that had once ornamented the foyer of Amy

Langford's beautiful bungalow, came crashing down on George's shoulder and sent him reeling against the wall of the house, but Nancy's quick grasp of his arm had saved it from falling straight onto his head.

Bob Merry, about to kneel down beside Mrs. Ramsden, looked up at the sound of the crash and a wooden footstool fell into his face, blackening an eye. The sharp leg cut into his temple and he staggered, but righted himself just in time to dodge the burning cushion that was the next object to come down. It fell on the gravel about a yard from where Mrs. Ramsden lay, and continued to burn.

By this time all four of them, George and Nancy, Bob and Mr. Fisher, were crouched against the wall of the house immediately underneath the broken balcony. Another cushion came down in flames, but Mr. Fisher was able to kick it to a safe distance. At least they were protected from any object coming on top of their heads, but it was only a very temporary refuge. And Mrs. Ramsden still lay there on the gravel, motionless.

"We must get to her," muttered George. His arm hung limply; he was clearly in pain.

"No!" said Nancy vehemently. "I'm sure she's dead. And we'll be lucky if we save ourselves."

There was blood streaming from the cut on Bob's face. "That ought to be seen to," said George. "If we could get along the wall here. . ."

"No!" cried Nancy again. "We're safer where we are."

"The fire brigade can't be long," muttered Mr. Fisher, hastily jumping back against the wall as a television set crashed within inches of his foot, sending splinters of glass and plastic in all directions.

"How does she do it?" cried Bob.

"Strength of madness," said George. "But it must take her a few seconds to drag the things to the window, so after the next one we'll have a short time of grace, and ought to be able to get to the corner—"

He was interrupted by a scream from Nancy. A sheet in flames was hanging from the balcony and the slight breeze was blowing it towards her head. At the same moment Mr.

Fisher, seeing Sue and Mrs. Fairfax appear round the corner
of the house, cried out to warn them.

"Keep away! Don't come any nearer!"

Sue obeyed him and stood still, but Mrs. Fairfax,
catching sight of Mrs. Ramsden lying on the ground, took a
few steps forward. The burning sheet broke loose from the
balcony rail and floated towards her. A tongue of flame
caught her thick wavy hair. She did not at first realise that
she was on fire, although several voices shouted at her.

Then she put a hand up to her head and the horror of her
face showed that she had understood.

"Roll in the grass!" shouted George. "Round the
corner!"

Mrs. Fairfax disappeared from view.

"Sue! Listen, Sue!"

George's voice was still firm, but Nancy, holding his
uninjured arm, could sense the effort with which he spoke.
This last incident had shaken them all. They were beginning
to lose their nerve, their power to decide.

Sue Merry stood with her face peeping round the corner
of the house.

"Phone the police!" shouted George. "Tell them there's
fire and a woman gone berserk."

Sue nodded and disappeared. George sagged against
Nancy's arm.

"D'you think that's the end?" she whispered. "There's
been nothing thrown down for some time now."

"She must be burnt herself," muttered Mr. Fisher.
"Perhaps she's collapsed."

There was a moment of total silence, and then Bob gave a
great howl.

"No! She's got out over the balcony and through the next
door flat. She's free—she's loose in the house! And Sue's in
there phoning! Sue! Oh God, Sue."

He ran to the corner of the house, leaving a trail of blood
on the gravel. After a split second of shock, the others
moved after him, Mr. Fisher in the lead, Nancy and George
following as quickly as the latter's failing strength would
allow.

The foyer of Digby Hall was filled with smoke, thickest on the first-floor landing, less dense on the ground floor. Mr. Fisher was held up by a fit of coughing when he reached the porch, and Nancy and George caught up with him. On the little Indian rug just inside the front door they all three stood gasping and staring with burning watering eyes at the scene in front of them.

The swirling smoke first concealed and then revealed three figures, frozen as in a tableau. Bob was the nearest, with his back to them and his hand grasping the back of a chair. It looked as if he could barely stand and was propping himself up. His other hand reached out towards Sue. She was several feet away from him, crouching over the telephone table at the bottom of the stairs. The receiver was in her hand, nowhere near her face. Her head seemed to be shrinking into her shoulders; her mouth was open, her eyes staring in horror.

A few inches away from her head, waving about and blocking her way of escape, was what looked like a flaring torch. It was a mop head, at the end of a long handle which was balanced across the bannisters. The smoke shifted to show the face of the woman who held the handle of the burning mop. It was blackened like the face of a miner, shining and greasy with sweat. The grey hair was full of black ashes. Only the eyes were light. They looked at the girl and then at the boy.

"If you move she'll go up in flames."

The voice was joyous, triumphant, exultant.

The burning mop quivered and a shower of sparks fell on the girl cowering beside the table. She dropped the telephone and clasped her arms around herself, writhing and trembling. The boy let go of the chair and staggered forward a step. The burning mop was swung round towards his face, sending out more sparks so that he involuntarily fell back.

They must rush her, thought Nancy in an agony of impatience and suspense. If Bob could grab at her feet through the bannisters, it would give Sue a chance to get away. It could be done, but it needed decision and nerve. And neither of the young people retained any such powers.

The girl was paralysed, hypnotised—beyond action or thought. The boy was weak from his own shock and injuries and the fear of making things worse.

Nancy heard Mr. Fisher mutter something and felt, rather than saw, that he had moved towards the door of Mr. Horder's old flat. George Cunningham was making little sounds of distress. He could do nothing; his right arm was useless. The fire bridgade would arrive at any moment, but it would be too late. Someone must rush in before the last of the burning mop was dropped on the girl's head.

The smoke was thickening again. Under its cover Nancy moved swiftly and quietly to the foot of the stairs, where she remained for a moment with her back pressed against the wall. Amy was standing on the third or fourth step from the bottom, and Nancy didn't think she had yet seen her. The mop handle was in her left hand; the wooden stick itself was now burning. She'd have to drop it soon in any case. But in her right hand Nancy now saw for the first time that she was holding what looked like a metallic object, brass or copper. A doorstop perhaps. To drop or throw when she had finished playing with fire.

Nancy thought quickly, edging herself up the stairs. She could grab at Amy's legs in a sort of rugger tackle and thus immobilise her, but then the burning strands would certainly fall into Sue Merry's face and the girl would not have the sense to act quickly to protect herself. Better to grab at the arm, or even at the end of the handle itself.

Without even knowing that this was what she had decided, Nancy leapt forward. One hand caught the wooden handle, the other caught the wrist that was holding it. There was an animal howl and Nancy felt a sharp pain in her leg. Amy was kicking at her with the heel of her shoe. The pain was numbing; Nancy gasped but kept her hold on the mop and on the arm.

Burning strands fell on the bannisters and over the edge of the stairs. Nancy saw the girl's upturned face: she had made no attempt to move.

"Bob—get her away!" she shouted. "I can't hold on much longer."

She had the impression of movement, but a great gust of smoke came from the now burning first-floor landing, blinding and choking her. Her numbed leg would barely hold her; the grip of her hands was weakening. And then came a crashing blow on the side of her head. It did not knock her unconscious: the brass doorstop, she thought, quite calmly and clearly. But her fingers momentarily lost their grip. Amy's hand, both empty now, came up at her face. Nancy flung her arms round Amy and held her close so that the clawing hands moved helplessly behind Nancy's back for a moment before coming up to tug at her hair.

But Nancy was the taller. Her own hands got a grip on Amy's hair, pulled and pulled, pulled the head back, back and back, felt the fingers that were tugging at her loosen, felt the body slacken, went on pulling, heard grugling sounds in the throat, and went on pulling.

It seemed to last forever. I'm killing her, said a little voice quite calmly and dispassionately in Nancy's mind. I'm killing her.

But there was life left in her adversary. The foot moved and the heel jabbed viciously at Nancy's instep. She swayed and lost her grip on the woman's hair. They clutched at each other and swayed together. And then they fell, still hideously embracing.

Before she lost consciousness Nancy heard the shrill screech of the fire engine.

11

"I won't wait another hour," cried Nancy three days later. "Not another minute. If I'm well enough to be allowed out of hospital, then I'm well enough to be told what's happened."

"All right," said George laughing. "Just give me time to collect my thoughts. After all, I'm still a bit of a convalescent myself."

His right arm was in a sling. Nancy carried no bandages, but there were marks of bruises on her face and neck and hands. Her headache had died down to a dull throbbing, but she still felt bruised and battered all over. Miraculously they had both escaped serious burns. They were seated in front of a coal fire in Mrs. Gurney's sitting room, and Mrs. Gurney's daily woman had just brought in a tray with coffee and biscuits.

"I don't know how I'm ever going to thank her properly," said Nancy. "I wish I'd never made those nasty remarks about her."

Mrs. Gurney had indeed proved a most kind and generous friend. Disaster seemed to bring out the very best in her. She had opened her house to all the survivors of the

Digby Hall catastrophe, and both George and Nancy were invited to stay there until they were well enough to find another home. It could have been embarrassing, in view of the much rumoured interest that Mrs. Gurney took in Dr. Cunningham, but Mrs. Gurney had coped with that too. Without causing anybody embarrassment, she had somehow or other succeeded in making it plain that the rumour was completely unfounded and always had been. Mr. Gurney was very satisfied with her circumstances and had not the slightest desire to marry again. What Mrs. Gurney very badly needed was an outlet for her abundant energy, and this the Digby Hall disaster had given her.

"She's loving every minute of it," said George, but he did not say it at all unkindly. "I think the only way we can thank her is to let her go on organising us."

"She can organise me to her heart's content," said Nancy. "I don't feel as if I ever want to make any decisions again."

"Except to bully me into going over the whole drama."

"That's different. If you don't tell me I am going to die of curiosity. Have you collected your thoughts yet? You didn't have concussion, did you?"

There was a note of anxiety in Nancy's voice. George shook his head. "No. Only my arm. Thanks to you, Nan."

"Well, what about Sue? Do hurry up, George."

"I think you probably saved her life too," he replied slowly. "If you hadn't tackled Mrs. Langford at that moment she'd have thrown the doorstop on Sue's head."

"But how is she? Was she badly burned?"

Again George shook his head. "The physical injuries weren't very severe. But it's going to take her a long time to regain her balance of mind. I feel terribly bad about Sue Merry, Nan. We shouldn't have let her go through that ordeal, but with time and a complete change of scene she ought to improve. She's staying with her mother. Bob is going to join them later. He's staying on in what is left of Digby Hall. They got the fire under control before it had done much damage in the warden's flat, and he offered to stay on the premises for the time being, until the insurance position is cleared up. He looks as if he has been in a prizefight, but it's not serious. And he's determined to carry on with his studies. And to look after Sue. He's got his work cut out, that young man, but I reckon he'll pull through."

"I think so too," said Nancy, "and I'm glad Sue is right out of the way. I had the feeling that Mrs. Langford was singling her out for the worst."

"Because she was the most vulnerable, the easiest to hurt. Yes, I think that's true. It was very nasty. Very nasty indeed." George's ruddy face looked sombre, and then he smiled and went on: "Let me tell you some brighter news. Mrs. Fairfax is none the worse—only minor burns on her hands and neck and a somewhat lopsided hairstyle. She and Ernest Fisher went to fetch blankets and other first-aid articles while you were doing your heroic act. Ernest wasn't hurt at all. Heaven knows how he escaped, but he did. He's gone back to his own flat and is up to his eyes in paperwork. I don't envy him dealing with the insurance, but he's in his element there. Just as Mrs. Gurney is in her element looking after the invalids."

"Did they manage to salvage any of our belongings?" asked Nancy. It was the first time she had thought about this. Possessions seemed so unimportant compared with the threat to human life.

"I'm afraid both your apartment and mine suffered quite badly," said George. "Bob's been trying to sort things out a bit and I shall help him as soon as I'm less feeble. The chessmen didn't suffer." George beamed at her. "We'll have a game this evening if you like."

They were silent for a moment, resting and thinking and adjusting themselves. Rain beat against the windows. Autumn was turning to winter. Mrs. Gurney's daily woman came in to collect the tray and to ask if a fish pie would do for their lunch. They were to be on their own because Mrs. Gurney was in London for the day.

"I can't seem to take it in," said Nancy when they were alone again. "It's all so unreal. Like a dream."

"More like a nightmare. But it happened all right."

"Mrs. Ramsden," said Nancy, suddenly remembering.

"She'd fallen from the balcony and she was lying there on the path. And we tried to get to her but couldn't. Was she dead?"

"She was dead. She was killed by the fall."

"Oh dear, oh dear." Nancy put a hand to her head. The throbbing was growing more painful. "We should have warned her. Oh George, what a terrible series of errors and omissions!"

"I think we just have to accept it, my love. We must try not to blame ourselves. We all did our best in the circumstances. No one can do more than their best."

"I suppose not." Nancy screwed up her eyes. "It's easy to be wise after the event. And after all, we'd only suspected her of killing Mrs. Graham and Mr. Horder and of persecuting Sue. We didn't know for sure. We didn't know she was going to go so horribly mad . . ." Her voice faded away. "I suppose she started the fire herself," she said presently.

"It looks possible. There may have been spirits spilt on the carpet, which could have helped it spread quickly."

"And Mrs. Ramsden—?"

"Too drunk to notice, I suppose, until it was too late."

"D'you think she pushed her off the balcony?"

"Probably. There's no means of proving it. Any more than anything else can be proved."

"I suppose not." Nancy rubbed her forehead again. Then she dropped her hand and looked a little brighter. "But at any rate, it's all over now. What's done can't be undone, but at least she can do no more damage."

George did not reply. He leant forward and put his left hand on Nancy's as it lay on the arm of her chair, and looked anxiously into her face.

"She can do no more damage," repeated Nancy slowly, "if she's dead." She paused and looked at George, and suddenly her hand began to tremble and her voice shook too as she went on. "If she's dead . . . do you mean, are you trying to say . . . oh my God! Oh George, no. Oh no. This is not to be borne." She steadied her voice. "Are you trying to tell me that Mrs. Langford is not dead?"

He nodded, watching her closely. "That's why I wanted to be sure you were well enough to hear the news."

Nancy fell back in her chair and closed her eyes. "I'd hoped it wasn't I who killed her," she whispered at last. "But I did hope—God forgive me, but I did hope—she was dead. From the fall. From her burns. She must have been badly hurt."

"She had some second-degree burns," said George. "She had concussion—no worse than yours. And severe bruising. About the same as yours."

Nancy moved her head from side to side as if she were in great pain. "So it was all for nothing. It'll happen all over again."

"No. It won't happen over again. It mustn't."

Nancy opened her eyes. "Where is she? In gaol?"

"She's in a very expensive private mental home."

"Oh God, oh God." Nancy moved her head again. "Why isn't she in prison? Why haven't they arrested her?"

"On what charge?"

"Starting a fire, pushing Mrs. Ramsden off the balcony, throwing things down on our heads, threatening Sue."

"It is by no means established how the fire started. Mrs. Ramsden could quite easily have fallen from the balcony in her attempt to escape the fire. Mrs. Langford, beside herself with panic, could have thrown things out of the window with some crazy idea of salvaging her belongins. Burns and shock and mindless panic could account for all her subsequent behaviour. People do terrible things when they are afraid and trying to save themselves. They push people out of lifeboats, trample other people underfoot. It's horrible, but they are not charged with murder."

"So there is no charge made against her?"

"At the moment, no."

"I can't bear it," said Nancy, falling back with closed eyes.

"I said, 'at the moment,'" said George. "The police are working with the insurance company investigators. And Clement Horder's death has not been forgotten. We'll have to hope that some piece of evidence comes to light that is conclusive."

"By which time she'll have recovered from her burns and been let loose to murder ten more people," said Nancy bitterly.

"I don't think that's likely to happen."

"Why not? It's happened before. She'll put on her pathetic victim-of-circumstances act. Poor little woman." Nancy adopted a simpering, mincing voice that had real viciousness behind it. "Such a shock to lose her gentleman friend in that dreadful accident—and then the fire. No wonder she was beside herself and behaved so oddly!"

"Yes, I'm afraid that will be the line," said George.

"You mean it's already started? That's the way she's dealing with enquiries?"

He nodded.

"She's going to get away with it." Nancy held both hands to her head. The pain was beginning to rage again; it was almost as bad as it had been when she first recovered consciousness. But it was not a purely physical pain. It contained frustration and fury and helplessness and despair such as she had never experienced in her life. She had always thought of herself as a steady, reasonable sort of person. She would never have believed that she could feel like this. It frightened her. She wanted to explain it to George and ask for his reassurance, but the words came out differently from what she had expected.

"I could kill her," said Nancy Pick with chilling calm. "In fact, if I get the chance I am going to kill her. Yes I am, George. It's no good looking at me like that. I was brought up to believe in the Ten Commandments and I do believe in them, but I believe there are exceptions. If a dog runs mad and is a danger to life, then you shoot it. I believe Amy Langford should be destroyed like a mad dog, and if the law cannot or will not do it, then I shall do it myself."

"You don't mean that, Nan."

"I do mean it." Her calmness had gone and she was banging her fists against her temples, as if by worsening the pain she could somehow make it less intolerable. "Somebody has to rid the world of that—of that evil woman."

There was a silence. George looked away. Instinct and his feeling for Nancy told him that it was better at this moment not to interfere. After a while she regained her composure and apologised for the outburst.

"I think I know something of how you feel," he said, "but I'm going to say something that may annoy you. If so, I'm sorry. But it's to be truth between us, Nan. Always truth. Isn't it?"

"Of course."

"Then I have to confess I do feel some pity for Mrs. Langford. Oh, I don't mean the sort of obvious pity she'll be playing for," he added hastily as Nancy made an impatient gesture. "Nothing to do with the pretence and the falseness. I think it's true pity that I feel. I don't know how to explain. I mean, it seems to me that she has missed so much. I m-mean"—he was stammering slightly in his eagerness to be understood—"I mean she's never been like a real person at all. She's the sort of woman who's always acting a part, is never herself. It's more common among women than men, isn't it? Men seem to be able to accept themselves and be themselves, but a lot of women seem to think they have to be something they aren't. Oh damn it, Nan. I know exactly what I mean, but I'm so bad at explaining. I wish you'd help me."

"I don't know that I can help, but I'm beginning to get your point. I can't feel pity for her, but I do see your point."

"I thought you would." George Cunningham sounded relieved. "You see, you're so very real yourself. That's why I love you, Nan. But I don't suppose anybody has ever loved Amy Langford. They may have spoilt her. Given in to her. But never really loved her. And that's a terrible thing. To go through life without ever having been really loved."

"You'll have me weeping in a moment," said Nancy with a smile. "But I won't pity her. She's a vicious crazy murderess, and she'd be better dead."

"I'm not asking you to pity. I'm just asking you to try not to feel murderous yourself. It's not like you. It's as if she'd dragged you down to her level."

"I don't think I feel quite so murderous now," said

Nancy. "You're very clever, George. Quite a diplomat. Did you know you were very subtle and clever?"

Dr. Cunningham looked very pleased with himself. "I think I'm improving," he said. "And now I'm going to tell you something that I think really will comfort your a little."

"Why you believe Amy Langford isn't going to do any more damage," said Nancy promptly.

"Yes. It's because of Jonathan. Her son. Fisher and I both had a talk with him. Nothing was said openly, but we both had the very strong impression that Jonathan Langford is under no illusions about his mother. He's an unpleasant sort of fellow, but he's not a psychopath and he's a reasonably law-abiding citizen. He started off with trying to blame us for not letting him choose the nurse-companion for his mother, but he soon changed his tune when we dropped a hint about her behaviour to Sue. He'll hush up everything he possibly can, of course, and if there is any suggestion of making any charge against her, which isn't likely, then he'll plead insanity. And he'll keep a very close watch on her. I'm sure of that."

"You mean she'll be shut up in some private mental clinic for the rest of her life?"

"I think that's what Jonathan will have to do."

"But she might still break out," said Nancy. "Or start attacking the staff."

"They're used to dealing with that sort of thing. They have their methods," replied George.

"Oh dear. Now you really are beginning to make me feel sorry for Amy Langford. Not exactly sorry, but rather disturbed. She could live another fifteen or twenty years. What a horrible sort of twilight existence."

"She'll be a lot more comfortable than she would be in Broadmoor," retorted George practically.

From the outside, Heron House had something of the appearance of an exclusive country hotel. It was about a mile and a half from the nearest village and was a well-proportioned, two-storey building that had once been a rectory. An annex had been built on at the back that blended in well with the mellowed brick. It was surrounded by a lawn and a thick beech hedge. The entrance to the premises was through high wrought-iron gates. It was a very private and secluded place.

Jonathan Langford parked his Rover in the drive, as near to the front door as he could get. While he waited for someone to answer his ring he turned up his coat collar against the cold lash of the rain that was penetrating into the porch. It was a raw and cruel day.

The woman who opened the door remarked on the weather. She was dark and middle-aged and wore a pale blue overall. Her voice and smile were correct but contained no warmth.

"Would you like to go straight to Mrs. Langford, or would you prefer to see Matron first?" she asked.

"I think I'd better see Matron," replied Jonathan.

"I'll go and tell her you're here, then. Perhaps you would like to wait in here." The businesslike smile came and went as the woman pushed open a door.

Jonathan sank down into a low chair next to a coffee table on which lay copies of *Country Life* and various travel magazines. The walls and carpet of the room were shades of blue. Some reproductions of abstract paintings hung on the walls, and on the windowsill was an elaborate arrangement of dried flowers. The central heating was turned up very high, and yet Jonathan shivered as he sat staring with unseeing eyes at the big bowl of honesty and everlasting flowers. This place gave him the horrors. It cost his mother's entire pension and a large chunk of his own income. The writing of those enormous cheques and the making of these horrible visits seemed to stretch on forever, on either side of him, like the walls of a tunnel. It was as if he was trapped in some modern problem play.

The waiting room was like some sort of limbo. He really didn't know why he had asked to see the Matron. They would have nothing to say to each other that had not been said on the previous visit. He didn't even like her. She was a somewhat larger version of the woman who had opened the door: correct, omnipotent, unassailable. But he was com-

pletely in her hands. The thought of having to look for
somewhere else to put his mother made him shiver and
sweat.

He glanced at his watch. Twenty to three. He would
certainly have to leave not later than half-past, and by the
time he had had a little chat with the Matron there would not
be very much time left to sit with his mother. Half an hour
perhaps. Surely he could endure half an hour of it. If only
they would offer you a drink. If only he'd had the sense to
order another whisky at the pub that was a few yards down
the road, the nearest building to Heron House. He slipped
his hand inside his coat and felt an inner pocket. There was
a flask of brandy there. But the woman might come in at any
moment, and he could hardly say that he was taking a nip
because he felt cold.

Reluctantly Jonathan withdrew his hand and looked at his
watch again. How slowly the minutes went by. Ten minutes
with the Matron and half an hour with his mother. It was not
very much in a lifetime of hours and minutes, and yet every
second that passed made it seem more intolerable. It was
like being in the dentist's waiting room.

"Would you like to come now, Mr. Langford?" said the
cool uninterested voice.

Jonathan had not even heard the woman enter. He had
been sunk deep in his own hell of time stood still. Matron's
office was very like the waiting room, except that it
contained a shiny steel desk and a filing cabinet, and instead
of dried flowers there was a large vase of hot-house roses.
That's where our money goes, thought Jonathan savagely.

"Good afternoon, Mr. Langford," said Matron.

"Good afternoon," said Jonathan.

"Not a very nice day, is it?"

"Not very."

"But we can't expect much else at this time of year."

"No. I suppose not."

Jonathan took a grip on himself. Time seemed to be
standing still again, and if he didn't make an effort to break
out he would be caught up in this inane conversation
forever.

"How is my mother?" he asked.

"Very much the same. I'm afraid there have been more of these attacks of depression and anxiety, but as you know, we are doing our best to control them."

She paused for Jonathan to express his gratitude and appreciation of all the skilled medical attention for which he was paying through the nose.

"There is one matter, though, that is causing us some concern," said Matron.

Jonathan felt a chill sickness. What was going to come next? Had his mother turned violent? Attacked one of the staff? Tried to set the place on fire? Was he going to be asked to move her? Or warned that he would have to move her unless . . .

"The drugs that we are giving in order to relieve the distressing symptoms," said Matron, "are very effective and, fortunately, the side effects are not very serious. But there are certain foods and drinks that must on no account be taken by patients on those drugs, since the combination is fatal. The food is no problem. Naturally the diet is planned to avoid the foods in question. But difficulties have arisen over fluids. All alcohol, of any kind whatever, is strickly forbidden to patients receiving this sort of medication. Even a trifle with sherry in it has to be avoided. I cannot stress too much that alcohol is absolutely forbidden."

She paused to look at Jonathan sternly.

"I quite understand," he said. "But surely there should be no difficulty in ensuring that my mother does not take any alcohol?"

"There ought to be no such difficulty, I agree. My staff are as reliable and trustworthy as any staff can be expected to be nowadays. Nevertheless, we discovered a small bottle of gin in your mother's room. Fortunately, it had not yet been opened. All the staff deny any knowledge of it."

"And what does my mother say?"

Jonathan waited with some interest for Matron's reply. Deep in his own personal hell something seemed to be stirring. The walls of the tunnel were still there and time still seemed to be endless, but nevertheless something was stirring. A seed under the hard soil of winter.

"Mrs. Langford," said Matron with a slight curl of the lip that Jonathan found very offensive, "naturally knows nothing about it either and was very surprised to find it was there."

"Well, and how do *you* think it got there?" Jonathan spoke quite abruptly. "I take it you are not suggesting that I am feeding my mother illicit gin?"

"Certainly not, Mr. Langford. Naturally, you would never do any such thing."

"Then who gave it her? She doesn't go out, does she?"

"Only into the garden when it's fine enough."

"Not to the pub?"

Matron lifted her nose and did not deign to answer.

"I supose she could get down to the pub," went on Jonathan thoughtfully. "It's only a few minutes away. And you don't actually lock them in, do you?"

"Mr. Langford," said Matron very coldly, "this is neither a prison nor a mental institution. Certain measures have to be taken in some cases to protect our patients from their own weaknesses. Sharp knives, for example, are not allowed. Nor are patients permitted to go into the staff quarters. Nor have access to drugs or any food or drink. All reasonable precautions are taken. But our patients are never, repeat *never*, subjected to physical constraint of any kind. It is not our policy at Heron House to accept any patient whose condition might warrant such restraint."

"Then the old girl could have slipped out for a quick one," said Jonathan crudely.

He was becoming more and more reckless. The stirring had become much more than a germinating seed. It had turned into a great urge to press on, to move towards the light at the end of the tunnel.

"Have you asked them at the pub?" he said, but before Matron could reply he went on: "No, don't tell me. Of course you've asked them, and naturally they deny all knowledge of it."

"The—er—landlord," said Matron stiffly, "is not always very cooperative."

"You mean he'll slip the odd bottle to some of the poor devils who manage to get clear of here for ten minutes now and then, and then deny that he's done it?"

Matron's reply was dressed up in a lot of verbiage, but Jonathan guessed that he was not far from the truth.

"What about the other patients?" he asked suddenly. "Could one of them have done the job for her?"

Matron, in her most self-justifying manner, admitted that this was not impossible.

"There is a certain amount of contact between patients," she said. "It is not good for a patient to remain in complete isolation. But of course we never take anyone here who is not recommended to us."

"Highest references required, eh?" said Jonathan in an almost jolly manner. "Ah well. I expect some of them get very fed up with their lives. I don't blame them for seeking refuge in the bottle now and then." He got to his feet. "I'd better go along to my mother now, or I'll hardly have time left to see her."

Matron rose as well. She looked as formidably authoritative as before, and yet there was a subtle difference. Jonathan had emerged as the victor in the encounter. There was no explaining it or accounting for it, but they both knew it was true.

"As long as you understand, Mr. Langford," she said, "that we do everything that lies in our power to safeguard our patients and ensure their well-being. What we cannot guarantee is that nobody should suffer from a flagrant breach of the rules."

"That's all right, Matron," said Jonathan heartily. "I quite understand. Of course you do your best, but if people are determined to kill themselves, they will. I promise that I won't blame you if somebody should give my mother a swig of whisky and it has unfortunate results. I'll even sign a document to that effect. There! Would that ease your mind?"

"I hardly think it will be necessary to go to such

lengths," said Matron with a prim little smile. "Just so long as you appreciate our position."

"Then I'll say good-bye now and thank you. As it's getting so late, I'll have to rush off directly I've seen my mother."

"I won't keep you any longer. You know the way?"

"Yes, indeed. Thank you again, Matron. It's a great relief to know you are looking after her."

And Jonathan produced a smile that was every bit as meaningless as her own.

Mrs. Langford's room was in the annex at the back of the house. It was on the first floor, and at the top of the flight of stairs there was a little office and utility room in which sat a nurse. She was youngish and cheerful and she smiled at Jonathan as he went past. He raised his hand in a lighthearted wave. He recognised her from the previous visits. She was the nearest thing to a real human being in this ghastly place.

The door of Amy's room was pale green. Jonathan knocked and heard her faint response. He entered, and the horror of time stopped assailed him again. The room was large and well furnished. The divan bed was in an alcove. Another alcove, curtained, contained the washbasin and mirror. Amy was sitting in an armchair by the window. She was wearing a blue woollen dress and highheeled black shoes. Her hair was neat and her face had obviously been made up with some care. There was a magazine lying unopened in her lap. The television was on, with the sound turned low.

When Jonathan came into the room she looked up at him and he did not think he had ever in his life seen such an expression of malevolence on a human face as that he saw in his mother.

"Open the window," she snapped without any preliminary greeting.

"I can't, Mother. You know the windows don't open."

"It's hot in here. I want some air."

"I'll try and fix the air conditioner."

"That's no good. It's too draughty," she said after Jonathan had fiddled about with it for some time.

He gave up. There seemed little point in trying further.

"Shall I put your flowers in water?" he asked.

He had brought bronze chrysanthemums. They were fine blooms and had cost quite a lot.

"I don't want the goddamned flowers!" she screamed.

"Then what do you want?" he snapped back.

"I want a drink." It was a childish wail. Then she began to bang her hands on the arms of the chair. "I want a drink! I want a drink! Why can't I have anything to drink?"

"Your tea tray's here," said Jonathan, turning to the low table. "Shall I pour you some?"

"No." She glared at him. "Not tea."

Jonathan moved swiftly to the door, opened it, and looked out into the corridor. There was nobody to be seen. He shut the door again and moved across to where Amy sat.

"Mother," he whispered urgently. "I've got something for you. But we'd better get out of sight of the door."

She looked up with a glimmer of interest. He put a hand inside his coat and drew out the brandy flask. Her eyes widened and she got up and ran to the corner where the curtain covered the washbasin. Jonathan took out a handkerchief and wiped all over the flask and then put on his leather driving gloves and kept them on.

"Here you are, Mother," he said. "Don't worry about a glass. No need for manners here."

She snatched the flask from his gloved hand, unscrewed the top, and put it to her lips. He watched in some amazement while she drank almost half of it without a pause. Then she raised her head.

"I'd better take it now," he said. "You shall have more later."

He screwed on the top and slipped the flask into the pocket of his overcoat.

"Oh. I feel giddy," said Amy.

"Come and lie down then." He took her arm and led her to the bed. Its cover was pale green. She fell back against the cushions and he pulled off her shoes and lifted her legs up onto the cover. Her eyes had closed and there was a faint smile on her face.

"That was lovely. Thank you, Jon," she murmured, and did not speak again.

He moved across to the door and looked out. There was still nobody to be seen. Then he found a vase and placed the chrysanthemums in it, screwed up the paper in which they had been wrapped, and dropped it into the wastepaper basket. He felt very hot but quite calm. His watch said seventeen minutes past three. He had told Matron he would be leaving about half-past. That would be the very earliest that anybody came into the room. Far more likely that no one would come for another hour or more, when the patients were asked when they would like the evening meal. And if his mother looked as if she was quietly sleeping . . .

Jonathan found a rug and laid it over Amy. Her face was turned away from him and she made no movement. He looked down for a moment at the flushed cheek and then, on a sudden impulse, bent over and kissed her forehead.

"Good-bye, Mother," he murmured. "I hope it's worked. I know this is the way you'd have wanted it."

For a few moments he remained leaning over, trying to judge whether there was any smell of brandy about her. It didn't seem to him that it was very noticeable, but he opened the top drawer of the dressing table and found her scent spray. A few puffs on the skin of the face and neck would drown any hint of spirits. When he had done, he replaced the spray and left the room. As he came into the corridor he saw a door a little further along just closing. The nurse's room at the head of the stairs was unoccupied. There was a shelf with some vases and empty bottles on it just inside the door, high up on the wall, out of reach of any save a tall person.

Jonathan took the brandy flask from his pocket and placed it on the shelf, pushing it to the back. They won't find it just yet, he said to himself; and when they do, let them puzzle over it. Naturally, everybody will deny any knowledge of how it came there.

He walked down the stairs and out the side entrance. The icy rain was still falling relentlessly. He turned up his coat collar and hurried round to where the Rover stood in the drive. The front door was shut and there was no sign of life. Heron House was as silent as the grave.

By the time he had driven the first twenty miles of his journey back to London, Jonathan Langford had convinced himself that he had carried out a mercy killing.

"It's really a happy release," said Mrs. Gurney when she told George and Nancy the news. "I said so to Mr. Langford when he telephoned me, and he agreed."

George and Nancy agreed too. Ernest Fisher also agreed when Mrs. Gurney used the same phrase to him. Nobody seemed to want to say much more about it than that. But later on, Nancy said to George: "So you were right about Jonathan Langford."

"My dear, we can't possibly know what happened. Fatal mixtures of drink and drugs are very common occurrences."

"Not in expensive private clinics."

"Oh yes. They happen there too. People get visitors to smuggle things in."

"Supposing," said Nancy presently, "that you possessed irrefutable evidence that Jonathan Langford contrived his mother's death, but that nobody else suspected. Would you feel obliged to take some action?"

George was setting out the chess pieces and did not answer.

"Would you?" persisted Nancy.

"No," he replied. "I should certainly keep quiet."

"So should I. Are we very wicked?"

"It's funny you should say that. You were all set on murdering Amy Langford yourself not so very long ago."

"Oh, I've got over that, thank God. But I'm glad she's dead. And if Jonathan did help it on, then I'm glad about that too. It seems right that it should be kept in the family."

"Poetic justice?"

"That's right," said Nancy, moving forward her white

queen's pawn. "There's a sort of feeling of a Greek tragedy about it, I think."

"But even if Jonathan was responsible," said George presently, "he'll never do such a thing again. He's not the stuff of which murderers are made."

"I think we're about to have one of our arguments," said Nancy, smiling. "I would say that all human beings are the stuff of which murderers are made."